"What are you looking for?"

"Any other potential evidence to confirm my theory." Bryson noted the spot where Hercules had burrowed and thrust his shovel deep.

Five minutes later, Bryson abandoned his pursuit. The avalanche had buried any other evidence.

"What now?" Jayla asked.

"Let's return to your base and search through your recent avalanche documentation."

"Okay, let's—"

Hercules barked.

Seconds later, the sound of an engine roared through the area. Was that one of their teams returning? Or—

A shot boomed, spraying snow at their feet and answering his silent question.

"Get down!" Bryson shoved Jayla to the ground and covered her body with his.

This attack proved his suspicions.

Someone had turned the already dangerous mountain into a deadly one. His question was—why?

Darlene L. Turner is an award-winning author who lives with her husband, Jeff, in Ontario, Canada. Her love of suspense began when she read her first Nancy Drew book. She's turned that passion into her writing and believes readers will be captured by her plots, inspired by her strong characters and moved by her inspirational message. Visit Darlene at www.darlenelturner.com, where there's suspense beyond borders.

Books by Darlene L. Turner

Love Inspired Suspense

Visit the Author Profile page at LoveInspired.com.

ALASKAN AVALANCHE ESCAPE

DARLENE L. TURNER

LOVE INSPIRED SUSPENSE
INSPIRATIONAL ROMANCE

LOVE INSPIRED® SUSPENSE
INSPIRATIONAL ROMANCE

Recycling programs
for this product may
not exist in your area.

ISBN-13: 978-1-335-58756-5

Alaskan Avalanche Escape

Copyright © 2023 by Darlene L. Turner

For questions and comments about the quality of this book, please contact us
at CustomerService@Harlequin.com.

Love Inspired
22 Adelaide St. West, 41st Floor
Toronto, Ontario M5H 4E3, Canada
www.LoveInspired.com

Printed in U.S.A.

And this is the confidence that we have in him, that, if we ask any thing according to his will, he heareth us.
—*1 John* 5:14

Brenda and Diane, my besties.

I'm blessed to have you both in my life.

Love you xo

Acknowledgments

Jeff "TooTall" Turner, not only are you the inspiration for the pilot in this book but your uplifting spirit inspires me every day. Love you.

To my beta readers: Brenda, Louise, Sandra and Priscilla. Thank you for catching my mistakes and reading my books so quickly. You gals are the best!

Debb Hackett, thank you for naming Hercules! It fits him perfectly.

Thanks to the following people for answering my questions: Maryann Landers (on Alaska) and Laurie Wood (on the Canadian military).

Thank you to the Alaska Search and Rescue Dogs (ASARD) for answering my numerous inquiries on your amazing dogs!

To my editor, Tina James, and my agent, Tamela Hancock Murray, thank you for your continued support and encouragement. I appreciate you!

Most of all, Jesus, thank You for always hearing my prayers. I love You.

ONE

Rumbles beneath her feet increased with every pulsating heartbeat that consumed mountain-survival expert Jayla Hoyt's body. Her muscles tensed with a rush of adrenaline as a cloud of white powder filled the air, blocking the blue sky. She recognized the familiar whumping sound. Mounds of snow were collapsing—fast. "Avalanche! Take cover!"

But there was nowhere to run. Nowhere to hide.

White spots danced in her vision, masking themselves among the glistening snow's glare. She drew in a long breath to suppress the terror bull-rushing her nerves. *You're trained for this. You know what to do.* She motioned for the group who had gathered in the Ogilwyn Mountain Pass—which stretched from the Yukon on into Alaska—to hurry.

Being buried alive was not how this day would end.

Not if she could help it.

"Deploy your airbags. Roll to the side, and arrest yourself like I taught you." Jayla motioned to her golden retriever. "Hercules, cover!"

Her K-9 search and rescue dog responded to her strained command, barking as he scrambled after her. She prayed the others would escape the avalanche's deadly path. She deployed her airbag, covered her face with her hands and moved to the side, with Herc at her flank. Thankfully, everyone had the proper equipment, including beacons, probes and shovels.

A question rose as snow pounded around the team.

How had she missed the signs?

Jayla had checked the weather and mountain particulars before bringing the small group for a survival-training excursion on this cold, sunny February day. The conditions were good—so what had caused the mountain to respond by hammering them with tons of snow?

In addition to her search and rescue skills, she also taught different teams how to survive on the mountain. She'd set out with a group of two police constables; her team leader, Ethan Ingersoll; and Herc for an in-depth introduction to deadly conditions.

Nothing like learning firsthand. She'd planned on burying one of them to show the group Herc's excellent rescue skills. It was how she'd trained him.

"Jayla!"

Ethan's cry startled her. She turned her gaze and caught a glimpse of her leader as he shoved a constable out of the way, but not in time to escape himself. The snow thrust him through the air, and he went tumbling with the avalanche. The slide finally came to a pounding stop near where they'd set up camp.

"No!" Jayla tried to move, but a wall of snow blocked her path. *Lord, save Ethan. You know what he means to me.*

She and Ethan had butted heads when she first joined the joint US/Canadian Cross-Border Mountain Task Force—a group of skilled individuals comprised of former military, law enforcement park rangers, constables and search and rescue specialists. Their Canadian team's commander, Sergeant Grant Park, also led the federal police constables. Ethan supervised CBM's day-to-day duties. Their unit patrolled the Alaska–Yukon border, saving many skiers from the deadly winters and training others how to stay alive during the different seasons. However, Jayla and Ethan had bonded after almost dying in the wilderness two years ago. She now respected the older man's reckless attitude. His quick thinking had saved her life.

Would she be able to save him now?

She unhooked her radio and pressed the talk button. "Avalanche on Ogilwyn's Peak. Send all units. Beacons are lit." She gave Kerry Park, her roommate and dispatcher, their approximate location.

Her radio crackled in response. "You're closer to the Alaskan team," Kerry said. "Deploying them now."

She cringed. Would they send *him*—the park ranger who'd frozen in a rescue mission, causing a good friend to get seriously injured? She'd never forgiven him, but she would accept any help. Even his.

Right now she needed to free herself and Herc from the snow wall in front of them in order to find the others. Using her shovel, she broke free.

"Hercules, search!"

The dog responded by bounding through the snow, stopping to poke his nose into different locations in a triangle pattern.

"Team, call out!" Jayla cried, hoping to aid Herc in his search. Every second mattered on a mountain.

"I'm good," Constable Dana Spokene said.

Jayla turned left and followed the woman's voice. Dana had clung to a tree and now leaned against the trunk, brushing off snow.

"Stay there. Help is coming." Jayla followed Herc, plodding her way as best as she could in her skis. Thankfully, they were still on since she'd escaped the avalanche's deadly path.

Herc barked.

Her K-9 buried his head in the snow as he dug furiously, tail in the air, wagging in a helicopter spiral.

His indicator that he'd found something.

She skied to his location and dropped to her knees, pulling out her shovel. With Herc by her side, she dug until they reached the victim.

Constable Joshua Hopkins—the officer Ethan had shoved.

She tunneled out the snow around his face and freed all obstructions from his airway before checking his pulse. He was alive but not breathing.

Jayla threw up her mask and gave him five rescue breaths, then waited.

He coughed.

Jayla sat back on her heels, relief relaxing her tightened shoulders. "Thank the Lord you're okay. Hercules found you, just like I trained him." She patted Herc's head. "Good boy."

Herc barked, snuggled next to Jayla and kissed her face.

The thirtysomething constable eased himself up. "Thank you." His words came out breathless.

Two found. One left. Ethan.

She stood. They must find her boss. "Hercules, search!"

Once again, Herc bounded through the snow, heading in the direction where Jayla had seen Ethan tumble.

Jayla turned to Joshua. "You okay?"

"Better now. Ethan shoved me away. I still got buried, but it could have been a lot worse."

"Have you seen him since?"

"No." He pointed. "But I saw him fall down there."

Jayla's gaze followed the direction of Joshua's finger. Herc dug in the snow, his tail in the air. He'd found something—or someone.

"Ethan." Jayla plowed through the snow over to Herc

and shoveled, holding her breath at the same time. They only had minutes to find him alive.

Herc tugged on an object and pulled it from the hole he'd created.

Ethan's ski boot.

Jayla continued to dig.

However, Herc stopped, indicating to her that Ethan was not under the snow. If not, where was he?

Herc bolted.

Had he picked up another scent?

Jayla followed, pleading with God to save her boss.

Her K-9 stopped and barked wildly.

Jayla approached. "What is it, boy?"

Herc looked up at her, barked and returned his gaze to what had caught his attention.

That's when Jayla saw it.

Ethan's discarded ski.

And a deep crevasse.

Her boss and friend had fallen to his death.

"No!" Jayla dropped to the ground and looked into the dark opening as tears cascaded down her cheeks. "Lord, why?"

He'd taken so many people she cared for during her lifetime. She couldn't handle another loss.

Herc nestled in beside her as if sensing her sorrow. She leaned into him and sobbed.

Seconds later, he dashed away and continued to dig.

The team was all accounted for, so what had the dog found this time? Jayla brushed away her tears and stumbled over to Herc. "Buddy, what did you find?"

He dragged something out from a hole.

Jayla gasped. Her army knowledge told her exactly what Herc had found.

A blasting cap.

Every muscle in her body stiffened. Did that mean the avalanche was not an accident? Who had triggered it—and why?

Snowmobiles roared nearby, interrupting her silent questions. Help had arrived.

Jayla waved them over.

One rider dismounted and approached, removing his helmet.

Lord, not him.

Why did she know the joint task force would send the man she never wanted to work with again?

Give me strength.

Alaska park ranger Bryson Clarke read the contorted expression on Jayla Hoyt's face. She was not happy to see him, and he didn't blame her. The last time they worked together had not ended well. His delay in responding to a dangerous situation had cost her team member dearly. The mission had happened six months ago and still haunted Bryson today. He wished for a do-over, but he didn't have a time machine to make that happen. After attending counseling sessions to deal with his mistake, he was not only a better person but had also grown in his role as a law enforcement park ranger. If only he could prove his integrity to both Jayla and his father.

Bryson concentrated on the task at hand, drew in a breath and walked over to Jayla. "You okay? Everyone accounted for?"

Her bottom lip quivered, and her gaze shifted to a discarded ski boot.

Not good.

Bryson grabbed her arm. "What is it, Jayla? What happened?"

"Ethan is gone. He pushed a constable out of the way,

and the avalanche took him over the ledge and into a crevasse." Jayla squatted in front of Hercules, drew a ball from her pocket, and handed it to him. "This guy helped save the others."

Bryson smiled. Her love for Hercules—who'd made a name for himself by saving countless skiers and lost hikers—shone through. Jayla and Hercules had an undeniable bond. Even though Jayla and Bryson's tumultuous relationship had caused friction between other task force members, he respected her and the abilities she and Hercules brought to their unit. Their track record of saves proved their worth.

If only Bryson could prove his.

Bryson's partners, medic Chris Ramsay and rookie park ranger Faith Julian, approached the group. Ramsay and Faith had traveled together on one machine. Thankfully, their station in Faircord Junction, Alaska, wasn't far from Jayla's location.

"Hey, Jayla. Who needs medical attention?" Ramsay asked.

She rose and pointed to a man sitting nearby, who inhaled and exhaled heavily. "Constable Hopkins. He was trapped in the snow, and I gave him rescue breaths to revive him. Maybe you can take him back to our base."

Ramsay gathered his bag. "On it." He trudged toward the constable.

"Bryson, Herc also found this." Jayla held out a blasting cap. "I believe someone deliberately triggered this avalanche."

Bryson cringed and drew her aside. "Listen, let's keep this quiet for now. I'll tell you more after we get your team to safety."

Her eyes widened, but she held her composure and

turned to the other woman in her party. "Dana, you okay to ski back down?"

Dana nodded.

"We want to get you off the mountain in case other avalanches follow." Bryson turned to Faith. "You good to lead her down? Jayla and I want to stay here to inspect the area for our report."

"Of course." Faith raised her skis. "Dana, can you follow me? I'll lead you the rest of the way back to the station."

Ten minutes later, only Bryson, Jayla and Hercules remained at the avalanche site.

Bryson squeezed Jayla's shoulder. "I'm so sorry about Ethan. He was a good man. I remember you said the two of you were close."

Her gaze traveled to the ski boot. "Thank you. I still can't believe he's gone." Her voice quivered, revealing her devotion to her leader and friend.

"He died doing what he loved."

Jayla sighed. "He did."

Bryson held out his hand. "Can you show me what Hercules found?"

She passed him the object. "I'm guessing it's a blasting cap from dynamite."

He cocked his head. "How do you know about dynamite?"

Her expression clouded. "I'm ex-military."

Interesting. How had he not known that? After getting stranded together while on a previous joint rescue mission, they'd shared their backgrounds.

Well, you didn't exactly share everything.

"How long did you serve?"

"Ten years." She put her gloved hands on her hips. "Tell me why you didn't want the others to hear this conversation."

Right to business. It would take more than a conversation about her army days to get back into her good graces. "Let's keep this between us. I've been going over the avalanche reports along the Ogilwyn Mountains in Alaska, and I'm guessing if you checked yours on the Yukon side, you may find the same thing. There are inconsistencies noted why the avalanches started. Some valid, some not."

"Wait… You think someone is sabotaging the mountain pass?"

"I do. Conditions like today's didn't warrant the snowpack to collapse."

Jayla turned her gaze toward the crevasse. "You and I both know the mountains are unpredictable."

"Agreed. If it was only one avalanche, I wouldn't have dug deeper. However, we've had at least four in the past month that just didn't seem to add up. Two of those avalanches resulted in fatalities. Well, now three with Ethan."

"But why would anyone deliberately trigger an avalanche and kill innocent people?"

"That's what my leader asked when I took the evidence to him before he told me to drop any further investigations into my conspiracy theories. Said I was creating dissension among the team." Bryson examined the blasting cap and raised it in the air. "But this confirms my suspicions. Something fishy is going on along our joint mountain pass, and it's up to us to find out what."

"'Us'?" She pointed to him, then herself. "You mean you and I? Working together?" She crossed her arms. "Do you remember how well that went last time?"

"I can't tell you enough how sorry I am about hesitating that day. I still have nightmares about it." Bryson dropped the blasting cap into his backpack's side pocket.

Her eyes flashed. "Your *hesitation*, as you call it, put my best friend in a wheelchair."

He averted his gaze from her penetrating glare. Would he ever be able to see something other than disdain in her beautiful dark brown eyes? "I know. I've been dealing with the fallout ever since. But for the lives of everyone who skis on the Ogilwyn Mountain Pass on our borders, can we work together?"

"But why me? Can't you ask Faith, Chris or someone else from your unit?"

He chewed the inside of his mouth. "I don't trust any of them."

She inhaled sharply. "What? And you trust me? Why?"

"I can't explain. Just a gut feeling."

Jayla let out an elongated huff. "Fine, but I'll have to approve it with my lead—" Her voice trembled.

"Who's the next ranking member of your unit?"

Her gaze snapped to his. "Me."

"Good, then. It's settled. We keep our findings between us. For now." He shoved a pole into the snow to mark the exact spot where they believed Ethan fell. It would help when they returned to the scene. "Show me where Hercules found the blasting cap."

She gestured. "Over here."

Hercules followed his handler as the group made their way to an area close to where Bryson had seen the female constable sitting.

"What are you looking for?" Jayla asked.

"Any other potential evidence to confirm my theory." Bryson removed his shovel, noted the spot where Hercules had burrowed and thrust the tool deep.

Five minutes later, Bryson abandoned his pursuit. The avalanche had buried any other evidence.

"What now?" Jayla asked, tucking an escaped strand of hair under her helmet.

"Let's return to your base and search through your recent avalanche documentation."

She bit her lip. "I can't leave Ethan here on the mountain."

"Understood. We'll bring in a recovery team." Bryson walked over to where the crevasse started and peered down. "There's a wall of ice there. We'll go to your base and gather the special equipment we need. Sound good?"

"Yes. That will give Herc some time to recoup before I bring him out in these cold temps again."

Bryson didn't want to verbalize what he guessed they both were thinking. Finding Ethan on this mountain would probably not happen until a spring thaw.

However, he wouldn't dampen her hopes of finding the man.

"Okay, let's—"

Hercules barked.

Seconds later, the sound of an engine roared through the area. Was that one of their teams returning? Or—

A shot boomed, spraying snow at their feet and answering his silent question.

"Get down!" Bryson shoved Jayla to the ground and covered her body with his.

This attack proved his suspicions.

Someone had turned the already dangerous mountain into a deadly one. His question was—

Why?

TWO

Jayla's erratic heartbeat pulsated as she struggled to breathe under Bryson's weight. Gunfire continued to echo throughout the mountain range. Questions pummeled her mind. Who was shooting at them? Why? And where was Herc? *Lord, protect us. I can't lose my dog, too.* Right now, he was her only family. An odd statement since she came from a large one—eight children. Some of her family had distanced themselves from her after she went through the necessary process to leave the army, stating they didn't respect her decision. However, they hadn't known the entire story—a story she'd kept from everyone. Plus, if her coworkers knew of her failures, she'd be exposed as an impostor and proved unworthy. Something she struggled with every day.

Herc's bark brought her back to their precarious situation.

The roar from the snowmobile came closer. She must take cover and get to Herc. She pushed on Bryson's shoulders. "Can't. Breathe."

His tall, muscular frame shifted to the side. "Sorry."

She gazed right, then left, searching for her dog.

Herc flattened himself nearby.

"Good boy, Hercules." She crawled to him, keeping herself low. She would not make them both a target.

"He's coming back around." Bryson whipped out his

gun and aimed at the approaching masked rider, taking two shots.

One hit the man's shoulder, causing him to lose his grip on the weapon. It fell into the snow. The man clutched his wound and turned the machine around, abandoning his rifle and retreating in the direction he'd come.

"That was close." She hugged her K-9.

She would do anything for the dog who'd not only saved her physically but also brought her back from the depths of a dark pit in her life.

One she refused to fall into again.

To avoid it, she would never give her heart to another man. It wasn't worth the pain.

After Michael's suicide, she had plummeted into the abyss. She had questioned why God had allowed another suicide to happen to someone she loved. Her brother Kyle had taken his life years before. His death had changed their father into a man none of them recognized. Even their sweet mother.

"I think they're gone, but we need to get off the mountain. It's not safe with all of those booming shots." He trudged through the snow to her side. "Hercules okay?"

Jayla rubbed the retriever's body, searching for any signs of injury. None. She kissed his forehead. "You're good, my friend. Let's go." She rose to her feet.

Herc jumped up and barked, wagging his tail.

Jayla smiled at her pride and joy. "He's fine."

"I'm going to get that rifle. There may be fingerprints on it." Bryson started his engine and rode over to where they'd seen the weapon land in the snow. Moments later, he returned.

Bryson pointed to the back of his machine. "Will Hercules stay in the snowmobile rack? I don't want you skiing back down. Not with the shooter still out there. He could have an accomplice."

"Yes, Herc knows to stay inside." She bent down and rubbed the dog's fur, pointing to the rack. "Hercules, up."

Herc barked and hopped into the steel carriage.

"Stay low behind me." Bryson adjusted his position to allow room for Jayla.

She grabbed her ski equipment and straddled the snowmobile. She looped her poles into the wire-rack frame and then placed her skis on her lap, holding them with her right hand. With her left, she clung to the bar behind her. "Ready!" she yelled over the engine's roar.

The machine lurched forward, but years of riding experience anchored her in the seat. Growing up on the Hoyt Hideaway Ranch in Alberta had instilled her love for the wilderness and mountains. No wonder most of her family had worked in some type of park or search and rescue occupation. It was in their blood.

However, for Jayla, it took the tragedy she'd caused while serving in the army to drive her back to the mountains—a place where she found peace and comfort even among the dangerous wildlife, storms and poachers.

She'd take them over heavy artillery any day.

They hit a bump, and she jostled in the seat. After securing herself, she turned to confirm Herc was still safe in the rack. She chuckled at the sight of him.

His raised nose and open mouth proved he was in his glory. He, too, loved the fresh mountain air.

They made the perfect pair.

Ethan had always said that about the duo. Tears spilled down Jayla's cheeks at the thought of her fallen beloved boss. Bryson was right about one thing. Ethan had died doing what he loved. The mountains were his life. He claimed it had been the reason his wife left. He had spent more time in the wilderness than with her, and it was why he had warned Jayla about having a relationship when married to nature.

The two didn't mix.

Was that really true?

Not that it mattered to her. Michael's death solidified her resolve to remain single—forever.

Fifteen minutes later, Carimoose Bay's mountain rescue station came into view. Multiple buildings housed a ski chalet and lift, their K-9 team and handlers, search and rescue specialists, and emergency services. A chopper sat on a helicopter pad to the right.

Bryson parked alongside the other snowmobiles and shut off the engine. He took off his helmet and turned. "Remember, let's keep our investigation to ourselves right now until we know who we can trust."

She flinched as a thought tumbled through. Could she trust Bryson Clarke—the man who had failed her friend?

The scene from that horrible day entered her mind. The grizzly and her friend in a wrestling match as Bryson stood frozen at the forest's edge. If it hadn't been for Ethan stepping in and spraying the bear, Julie would never have survived.

Jayla gritted her teeth. Bryson's presence brought the pain plummeting back. She eyed the rifle in the ranger's hand and squared her shoulders, dismounting as determination steeled her resolve to piece together whatever was happening on her mountain.

And prove someone had murdered Ethan.

"I can't imagine anyone on my team being involved with something this heinous, but I will reserve my judgment for now." She turned to Herc. "Come."

The dog jumped down.

Not waiting for a response from Bryson, she sprinted

toward the station with Herc at her heels and placed her skis on the rack beside the door. She entered the building, stomping snow from her boots.

Bryson stormed inside, a scowl twisting his handsome face. "Please work with me on this, Jayla. For Ethan's sake."

You would *use that angle.*

She suppressed the words she wanted to utter. "You're right. What do we do first?"

He lifted the rifle. "Do you have anyone on your team connected to Forensics?"

Jayla placed her fisted hand on her hip. "I thought you didn't want me to involve anyone."

"Well, we need someone to check this into evidence and see what we find. Anyone you trust?"

"Yes. Constable Dana Spokene's husband works in Forensics." A question rose. "But can we bring her in?"

Bryson tapped his boot. "We tell her we found it on our way back down and need to find the owner. Their prints might be on it."

Jayla puckered her lips, pondering the scenario. "It might work, but it also might backfire on us. I don't want people thinking I'm not trustworthy. After all, I'm now an interim team leader here."

"But she's not technically on your unit, right?"

"Well, the constables liaison with CBM often, and I don't want to ruin that relationship. We need each other."

"We have to take the risk."

Herc barked, reminding her of his presence.

Jayla fished his ball out of her pocket and tossed it. "Go get it."

He bounded after his toy.

"First, I need to feed Hercules. You see if you can find Dana." Jayla pointed down a corridor. "She may be in the lounge." She headed in the opposite direction to the K-9 supply room. Their station housed three different search and rescue breeds—German shepherd, border collie and golden retriever. The three dogs had saved many lives.

Jayla halted at the sight of Ethan's office and swallowed the thickening in her throat. The reminder of his death sent tremors throughout her body, robbing her lungs of air. *Give me strength, Lord.*

She had to organize a search and recover expedition back to Ogilwyn Peak, but as the reality overpowered her, she doubled over, puffing out ragged breaths.

Ethan was gone, and they probably wouldn't find his body until spring.

She bolted upright. She might not recover her leader yet, but she would find the person responsible.

If it was the last thing she did.

After determining Constable Spokene's husband wouldn't be available to come to the station for a few hours, Bryson withdrew his cell phone. He had to reach out to his boss and explain why he and his colleagues hadn't checked in. Both Ramsay and Faith were consulting with other members of Jayla's team before heading back to Alaska. Bryson required more time to go over Jayla's records, but how could he request for his boss to allow him to stay without tipping his hand? He needed a story—and fast.

Bryson walked back into the hall and noticed Jayla sitting in Ethan's office. An idea formed, and he hit Supervisor Leon Thamesford's speed dial number.

"About time you called," the man blared in his rough, raspy voice.

Bryson braced himself for Thamesford's mood. The man was good at his job, but sometimes could be hard on his employees. "You're right, boss. Sorry for not calling sooner, but we've been busy." He explained the situation but left out certain details.

"Time for you guys to get back here. Stat."

Bryson flinched. The man's tone sailed through the airwaves. He meant business, but Bryson had to convince his boss to let him remain behind. "Sir, Chris and Faith are almost done. They will head back within the hour."

"Good. And you, Clarke?"

Bryson inhaled deeply. This man already didn't trust him, and what Bryson was about to do would widen the wedge of distrust. Exponentially. But it couldn't be helped. Lives were at stake, and Thamesford had already dismissed Bryson's theory of illegal activity. "Sir, Jayla needs my help in recovering Ingersoll's body. We discovered a wall of ice in a cavern where we feel he fell through. You're aware of my expertise in that area. I can help."

The man moaned. "Fine. We need to help our Canadian friends. Get back quickly, though. You're on thin ice, and not even your dad can help you this time." He hung up.

Right. It was bound to happen. The man didn't like that Bryson's father had helped him get onto the cross-border task force. Even though Lieutenant Trent Clarke had assisted him after Bryson announced his departure from the Alaska State troopers, his father wasn't happy about it. Another disappointment in Bryson's long list of failures in his father's eyes. *Dad, when will I measure up to your standards?* Bryson had struggled all his life to please his father but failed every time. No matter how hard Bryson tried, nothing was ever good enough for Lieutenant Clarke.

And Bryson's ex-girlfriend, Gabby Smith, had made matters worse when she accused him of accepting bribes while on duty with the troopers. Something he would never do. They'd exonerated him, but in his father's eyes, the embarrassment tainted Lieutenant Trent Clarke's name.

Bryson's grip tightened on his cell phone before he tucked it back into his pocket. He let out an elongated exhale.

"Well, well. Is the mighty Bryson Clarke having a bad day?" Chris Ramsay's words were laced with contempt.

The question was, what had Bryson done to deserve them? He thought he knew Ramsay, but lately the man had been acting strangely. Could it be because of the time when Bryson had challenged Ramsay on a call?

"Well, it hasn't been a good one so far." Bryson wouldn't take Ramsay's bait. He didn't have time to get into it. "Just talking to the boss. He wants you and Faith to head back. I'll be staying to help Jayla recover Ethan's body."

Ramsay leaned against the wall. "Oh, I see. I get it. She's cute. You're smitten."

Really? That's where you go? "I'm only helping her find her boss."

And that's all it would ever be. Yes, the mountain-survival expert was beautiful, but she hated Bryson. That wouldn't change.

Plus, Gabby's betrayal had cut too deep.

"I heard your conversation, and I think you're holding something back from our fearless leader. What is it?"

"What's what?" Faith popped around the corner.

Ramsay nodded toward Bryson. "This guy is keeping secrets. I'm aware of your investigation into these avalanches. Is that what this is about?"

"What investigation?" Faith asked.

Ramsay harrumphed. "He thinks they're not accidents."

Bryson had to end this conversation before the sudden conflict between them grew larger. He raised his hands. "I need to help Jayla. I have ice wall–climbing experience."

A half-truth. He had that knowledge, but he also wanted Jayla's help with going through the Yukon's reports.

Ramsay nudged Faith. "Plus, he's smitten with our Canadian task force member."

Faith's face contorted for a split second before she turned her gaze to a different focal point.

Bryson almost missed the look of contempt because he didn't know her that well, but it was clear. Why? She'd only been on the team for two months and had been assigned to Bryson to take under his wing.

What was he missing?

Before he could contemplate it further, Hercules bounded into the room, followed by the woman in question.

Bryson bent down and ruffled the dog's ears. "Did you have a good lunch?"

Hercules barked.

Nothing like a perfect distraction to steer them away from a tense conversation.

"What's going on here?" Jayla asked, glancing at each of them separately.

She knows.

Hard to hide anything from the astute woman.

"Clarke here is trying to tell us the reason he's staying behind, but we know the truth," Ramsay said, his mocking voice booming in the small room.

Jayla shrugged. "He's helping me organize a search and recovery team for my boss. What other truth is there?"

Smart girl.

Bryson suppressed the audible exhale he wanted to expel. "Did you contact the players involved?"

She raised a file. "Sure did. Shall we? Hercules, come."

The retriever followed her out of the room.

Bryson poked his finger in Ramsay's shoulder. "Told you. Have a little faith, man."

Bryson left the room without waiting for an answer, but not before catching the scowl on his coworker's face.

So be it.

He found Jayla in Ethan's office and plunked himself in a chair across from the desk. "Thanks for covering."

She tapped the file she'd been holding. "Let's get something straight. I'm not happy with going behind our team's back on this. We need to bring them in on it. If there really is illegal activity happening, they can help."

Even Jayla didn't believe him.

He slumped in the chair. "How can you say 'if' after what we just went through? Someone tried to kill us and Hercules."

Her facial expression softened before she grimaced and glanced at her dog. "You're right. It's just so hard to comprehend, and I don't enjoy deceiving people. I've had enough—"

She stopped.

He leaned forward. "Enough what?"

"Nothing. Never mind." She opened a laptop.

Had someone deceived her? Was that why she left the army? Answerless questions pounded through his head. But for now, her trust in him was all he required. "Jayla, I realize we've had a shaky past, but you can count on me. This time."

She frowned. "I hope so. I can't go through that again."

"Understood." Neither could he. His failure at not acting on the threat cost her friend dearly, and any self-respect he'd had.

It had taken months for him to feel good about himself again, and this was his way of proving it to his father, co-workers—and Jayla.

She clicked on the keyboard. "Okay, what date do you want me to search?"

He fished out his cell phone, opened his notes app and

gave her the first suspicious avalanche date he'd recorded, then three others.

He waited while she searched.

She nibbled on her bottom lip.

A habit he remembered from their last time working together.

Did she realize how cute that simple mannerism was on her beautiful face?

Stop, Clarke. Focus.

She whistled. "You're right. I see a questionable pattern here."

He flew from his seat and positioned himself behind her.

She pointed. "Look at these dates and weather patterns. Something's amiss. We definitely need to investigate."

"To answer your earlier question, I don't trust my team because I compiled some data and forgot it on my desk. When I ran back to get it, it was gone. Someone took it." He fisted his hands on his hips. "Ever since then, I've been keeping my suspicions to myself."

She leaned back. "I'm sorry for doubting you. Ethan was murdered, and I need to find out why."

He squeezed her shoulder. "We'll figure it out. We just need to keep it a secret from—"

An explosion rocked the search and rescue station, leaving no further doubts in Bryson's mind. It also dawned on him…

Someone knew they were investigating and wanted to scare them off.

THREE

Jayla shot out of her chair, her pulse throbbing in her head. Her beloved station was under attack. Had the suspect followed them here? But how? Bryson had wounded him. "That sounded like it came from beside our building." She gasped. "The kennel!" *Lord, help the dogs not be in there.* She snatched her coat and bounded from the room with Herc at her heels.

"Jayla, wait!"

Bryson's shout barely registered as she burst through the front doors. She wasn't thinking about her own safety but of the welfare of their precious dogs.

Heat stopped her in her tracks, then threw her backward.

Flames rose from the demolished kennel. She whipped out her cell phone and dialed 911, requesting firefighters to her location.

Herc barked and sprinted toward the kennel.

"Hercules, halt!" She couldn't let him go any closer.

The K-9 whimpered but obeyed.

She fell to the ground beside Herc and pulled him into an embrace.

"Jayla, I saw other dogs inside earlier." Bryson crouched next to her. "Perhaps none were in the kennel. How many are normally on active duty?"

"Three." She yanked her radio from her belt. "Philip, report. Where are Moose and Stella?"

She held her breath as she waited for a reply. *Please, Lord, help them be okay.*

"Both out on patrol with me," Philip said. "What's going on? I thought I heard a rumble."

Jayla's shoulders slouched in relief. "Our kennel was just blown up. Thank God they're with you."

"Where's Herc?" the K-9 handler asked. "What happened?"

"Not sure. Herc's with me." She eyed the destroyed building and then Herc.

One thing was for certain. Someone wanted the dogs stopped from searching—but for what? She eased herself to a standing position and rolled her shoulders back, tenacity taking root. It was her responsibility to keep their trusty friends safe.

"Take them to a secure location. Somewhere no one knows about." She knew the chain of command hadn't been established yet, but she didn't have time to play around. "Just in case."

"In case of what?" Philip asked. "Do you think someone did it deliberately?"

Bryson stood, placed his hand on her shoulder and shook his head.

"Not sure yet. Please do it." She clipped the radio back on her belt and addressed Bryson. "I hate keeping secrets. People will wonder about this explosion." Jayla bent down to kiss Herc's forehead. "Your buddies are safe."

He barked and snuggled closer.

Faith and Chris ran through the entrance, staring into the ruins.

"What happened?" Chris asked.

Bryson's eyes narrowed. "Why are you guys still here?"

Jayla didn't miss the harsh tone in his voice. She'd sensed tension in the air earlier, but didn't he get along with his team?

Chris walked into Bryson's personal space. "We were just about to leave, *boss*. Can I remind you of something? You're not our leader, and we don't take orders from you."

Bryson fisted his hands but kept them at his sides. "Thamesford gave me your assignment. Don't blame me."

A question rose in Jayla's mind. What had happened between these two to create such friction? It was clear they butted heads like two steers in a deadlock over territory.

Faith jerked on Chris's arm. "Come on. Let's go before these two totally spoil our day." She glared at Bryson and then Jayla, her expression hardening.

What? Faith was new to the team, and today was the first time Jayla had met her. How could she already have that much animosity toward her?

Faith gave Bryson one last look before stomping toward their snowmobile.

Aw... You have a crush on Bryson. A girl can read the signs. But why was she jealous of Jayla? Couldn't she sense the undeniable tension between them?

The snowmobile roared onto the path that would take the two back into Alaska.

Sirens broke through her thoughts and returned them to the situation at hand—where they should be.

A fire truck pulled into their parking lot, and firefighters jumped down before extending their hose to extinguish the flames.

"I'm sorry about all that, Jayla." Bryson nudged her toward the firefighters. "Let's talk to the chief."

"Wait. Clearly Faith has a thing for you, and for some strange reason, she thinks I'm a threat. She obviously doesn't know our past. But why the tension between you and Chris?"

Bryson zipped up his coat. "Let's just say he didn't agree on a call I made that put him in a poor light."

"You seem to have a habit of creating tension on a team."

"I assure you, it's not intentional. I really am a nice guy." He walked toward a firefighter, then pivoted. "And Faith doesn't like me in that way, and I'm certainly not interested." His gaze burrowed through her before he turned back toward the scene.

Like I care.

Or did she?

She shrugged off the question and followed Bryson, Herc at her heels. No time for relationship nonsense. She had a team to lead and dogs to protect.

Two hours after conferring with the fire chief, they still didn't know the cause of the explosion. Constable Spokene's husband had brought a team in to not only take the rifle Bryson had picked up but to also investigate the explosion. He promised to expedite the results.

Jayla and Bryson now faced the team they would take back to Ogilwyn's Peak to search for their beloved leader's body—a feat Jayla didn't relish. Ice climbing was dangerous. However, she required closure.

"Who put you both in charge?" Constable Hopkins asked. "Isn't Ranger Clarke from Alaska?"

Bryson's groan beside her revealed his mood.

Jayla stepped forward, attempting to curb any conflict. "My seniority makes me the highest-ranking team member here, so that does." She crossed her arms. "You can take it up with Sergeant Park later. I spoke to him earlier, and he okayed the chain of command until they can find a replacement. Is that okay with everyone?"

She stared at each of them separately.

Now was not the time to show how she really felt inside. If they knew that her stomach was twisted in knots and her legs threatened to wobble, they'd definitely have an issue.

The group nodded.

"Okay, good. We need to locate Ethan's body, but it won't

be easy." Her voice quivered, so she breathed in, taking a pregnant pause.

Bryson moved to her side, as if sensing her hesitation. "That's where I come in. I have experience in ice climbing, and we believe Ethan fell through a crevasse."

Thankful to him for grabbing the proverbial baton and coming to her rescue, Jayla clapped. "There's a storm moving in later today. Let's get ahead of it. You have your assignments—grab your equipment, and let's move out."

The group dispersed.

Pounding footsteps approached from the foyer, intruding on their conversation. Jayla turned at the interruption and sucked in a ragged breath. *Why is* he *here?*

Yukon park warden Dekker Hoyt smiled his lopsided grin—the one that always captured ladies' attentions everywhere he went and left a trail of broken hearts behind. The last time Jayla had seen him, they had a falling-out when she challenged him on his wayward tendencies. She longed for the close relationship they'd once enjoyed.

"Sister, how are you?" The towering warden hauled her into an embrace. "I've missed you."

Jayla bristled. "Why are you here, Dekker? This isn't your park."

"Well, good to see you, too, sis." He turned to Bryson and stuck out his hand. "Dekker Hoyt. You are?"

"Alaska State park ranger Bryson Clarke." Bryson returned the gesture. "Nice to meet you."

Dekker tapped his toe. "Oh. You're the infamous Ranger Clarke I've heard about."

Brother, not the time to stir up a hornets' nest. "Dekker, why are you here?"

"I caught wind of what happened to Ethan and wanted to help." He play-punched her arm. "Sis, you're not the only Hoyt who knows their way around the mountainside."

"Do you have experience in ice climbing?" she asked.

"Some. Why?"

Jayla motioned toward Bryson. "He does, and we're about to leave on a recovery mission."

"The crevasse isn't very wide, so I'll be the only one going down. However, I could use your help topside." Bryson zippered his jacket.

Great. That's all I need—a man I don't trust and a reckless brother. Not a good pairing.

"Let's go." Dekker headed toward the front exit.

Jayla grasped Bryson's hand. "Watch your back with my brother."

"Why?"

She hesitated, not wanting to speak unkindly of family. "Let's just say he's reckless. Anyway, I'm concerned about your plan."

"Jayla, I know what I'm doing." Bryson left the room.

Could she trust the man who had failed her in the past? She restrained the urge to harrumph.

Right now, she had to put her faith in Ranger Bryson Clarke.

Bryson accelerated his snowmobile, following Jayla's team through the wilderness to the area where Ethan had plummeted in the avalanche. Jayla and Hercules rode beside him on their own machine. He wasn't sure if it was because of their added gear or that she didn't want to be close to him. Bryson guessed the latter. He couldn't expect her to trust him after only being together for a few hours. It would take time.

Time they didn't have. If they were to understand whatever was happening in their joint Ogilwyn Mountain Pass, she had to put her faith in him. A question niggled his mind…

Would he ever trust himself again after the mistakes

he'd made in both trusting Gabby and not acting quick enough in the bear attacks?

His mother would tell him to give it over to God, but Bryson wasn't ready to go there. After being raised in an agnostic home, it was hard to reverse his thinking. Dr. Shannon Clarke had given her life over to Christ two years ago and continually begged him to go to church, a battle she had failed to win with her husband. Perhaps his mother was right—Lieutenant Trent Clarke and his son were both two stubborn peas in a pod.

Even though Bryson had said no to his mom, he allowed her to take his seven-year-old niece, Avery, to church. His sister, Ellie, would have wanted it that way. The thought of the vivacious little girl brought a smile to Bryson's frozen lips. She was the light in his world. After the tragic death of Ellie's husband overseas, Ellie had made Bryson promise that if anything happened to her, he'd become Avery's guardian. Ellie's death had instilled Bryson's fear of bears. They'd been on a campout when the grizzly attacked. Bryson was coming back to their site from fishing when the beast charged toward Avery, and Ellie intercepted his path, sacrificing her life for her daughter's. That was six years ago.

And her death still haunted him today.

He had failed to reach his sister after snatching Avery into his arms, taking her to safety.

Jayla slowed her machine, bringing Bryson back from the horrifying memory. One that would remain forever etched in his mind.

Bryson parked beside Jayla and killed the engine. He removed his helmet and assembled his gear.

The rest of the team arrived, including Dekker. Questions filled Bryson's mind about what Jayla had referred to earlier when it came to her brother. However, he couldn't speculate about it now. They had a job to do.

Constables Hopkins and Spokene unloaded shovels and other equipment.

Bryson examined the scene to ensure everything was still secure after the avalanche had pummeled Jayla's group earlier in the day. He searched for the pole he'd placed to mark the crevasse, but it was nowhere to be seen. How was that possible? He'd inserted it deep, and the weather hadn't changed. He bent over to investigate where he guessed he had put the marker and noted footprints in the snow.

More than his and Jayla's. He drew in a ragged breath and shot upright.

Someone else had been there since they'd left. Were they still hiding among the trees?

The hairs on the back of his head prickled, and he scanned the area. Suddenly, he had the overwhelming sense of being watched. But how? This part of the mountain wasn't normally populated by anyone hiking or skiing.

Jayla latched onto his arm. "What is it, Bryson? You look alarmed."

He pointed to the ground.

"Wait… Isn't that where you put in the marker?"

Hercules raised his nose in the air and barked.

Did he also sense someone nearby?

Bryson rested his gloved hand on his weapon. "I think we're being watched." He scanned the area once more, but nothing out of the ordinary stood out.

Hercules remained silent, which told Bryson that whatever they'd heard or detected was gone. An animal, perhaps, or his overactive imagination. He sighed and gazed upward. Darkened clouds kissed the mountain peaks. The storm was approaching faster than they'd expected.

"We need to move if we're going to attempt this search." Bryson pointed to the sky. "Storm's moving in."

"Let's make a plan." Jayla waved the team over. "Okay, time to execute your assignments. Constables Spokene and

Hopkins, conduct a search around where we found Ethan's ski boot. Look through the brush and trees. Dig through the snow. Hercules didn't alert to anything earlier, but we have to cover all angles."

The two constables nodded and picked up their shovels.

She turned to Bryson. "Okay, you take the lead on this part of the plan since you have the experience."

Bryson wiggled into his harness, fastening the required ropes and pulleys before addressing Dekker. "Use the pickets and create two T-slots to hook me up and anchor me. Pack them hard. We'll add a second rope onto you, so get your harness and axe because if something happens, you can self-arrest to hold me. Got it? No mistakes."

Dekker barked a sharp laugh before glancing at his sister and then back at Bryson. "I've been trained on that, too, you know." He left to grab the gear.

Bryson tucked an ice axe into a loop on his jacket. "Jayla, you help Dekker and monitor the weather for me. If it worsens, we'll have to abort our mission and get off the mountain. I'm not sure how deep the cave is, so our radios probably won't work. When I'm ready to come up, I'll tug on the rope."

After Dekker secured the line, Bryson added crampons to his boots. The spikes would assist in scaling the glacial wall. He checked his ice-climbing gear one more time before lowering himself into the crevasse.

The frozen, confined space radiated a chill that sent tremors spiraling into Bryson's bones despite his insulated gear. A thought rose…

Ethan wouldn't have survived long in these conditions. Even if he'd endured the fall, the freezing temperatures and ice walls would have given him hypothermia. For Jayla's sake, Bryson hoped they'd find him so she'd have closure. It wouldn't be easy, but not knowing was almost worse.

Bryson gingerly edged his way down, using his ice axe

and digging his crampons into the wall, relying on the tethered rope to keep him anchored. Minutes later, he came to the ice cave's floor. He shined his flashlight and made his way down a passage, his special boots digging into the icy surface. He took the bend carefully and stopped beside an object that had the CBM logo.

Ethan's backpack.

Bryson inched forward and examined the area. The bag teetered on the edge of another drop. Bryson peeked over the threshold, but blackness obstructed his view.

"Bry—storm—pick—up—leave—now." The cave hampered Jayla's message.

However, Bryson understood her broken warning. He snatched the bag and returned to the drop site.

After tethering himself, Bryson tugged on the rope.

Distant gunfire exploded topside.

Bryson's muscles tensed as his heartbeat hammered. "Jayla!" he yelled up into the crevasse.

Silence.

"Jayla, report!" Bryson's voice boomed in the narrow space. "Dekker?"

Where was everyone?

Bryson would need to rely on his ice wall–climbing abilities to get out of this darkened cavern, but a question remained.

What would he face once he reached the top?

FOUR

Jayla lay frozen in the snow as terror tightened her chest. She threw one hand over her head and the other over Herc, sheltering them both from bullets. Jayla and Dekker noted Bryson's tug on his line just as the first shot boomed. If more gunfire erupted, they'd risk setting off another avalanche. Where were the constables? Dekker? *Lord, where are You? Protect us.*

Herc whimpered beside her, and she brought him closer. "It's okay, boy. I've got you."

God's got you, Jay. Be still and let Him hold you.

Words her mother had spoken to her just after Michael had taken his own life filled her mind. Why now? Was God reminding her to stay still? To rely on Him?

She'd done that all her life, but after having to deal with the suicides of two people she loved, she struggled with her wavering faith. Plus, it was her fault Michael had taken his life. If only—

"Jayla!"

Bryson's blaring voice thrust her back to their situation. Had he climbed up the icy wall without their help? An inch of respect for him bubbled to the surface.

"Bryson, take cover. Shooter is nearby." She waited for more shots, but none came. "Are they gone?"

He raised his weapon, pointing it all around. "I don't see anyone, but the blinding snow isn't helping."

Jayla eased herself into a seated position, moving her

hands over her K-9's body, searching for any type of injuries. Seconds later, she brought him into a hug. "You're good, Herc. Love you, bud."

Ruff!

"How did you get to the top so quickly?" Jayla asked.

"I heard the gunfire, so I used my axe to help me move quicker. Plus, my boot crampons give me traction." Bryson dropped a backpack and put away his gun before glancing around. "Where's Dekker?"

"He was just here." She stood and peered through the snowstorm, pointing. "There!"

Dekker moaned as his blood turned the snow red.

"Dekker!" Jayla trudged over and fell beside her brother. "Are you okay?" She resisted the urge to shake her fist in the air. "Lord, haven't You allowed enough?" It would mortify her mother if she heard the words Jayla had just spoken.

Dekker winced and tried to sit. "I'll be fine, Jay. Got shot in the leg."

Bryson eased him back down. "Don't move. We need to get you to the station before you lose more blood."

The constables approached.

Jayla shot upward. "Where have you been? Someone shot my brother!"

Constable Spokene holstered her weapon. "We were kind of busy dodging bullets. I'll call it in." She withdrew her radio and walked away.

Bryson addressed Joshua. "We have to move now. The shooter—"

Herc made a beeline for the snow-packed trees and then sat, barking excessively.

Jayla's muscles locked at the sight of her K-9's erratic behavior. "What is it, boy? What do you see?"

He barked again.

Movement to the right caught Jayla's attention. "Someone is still out there, Bryson."

The ranger unholstered his weapon. "Stay here."

Joshua raised his 9mm. "I've got this."

"I'm an ex-trooper and trained. Let's do this together as a team." Bryson motioned for Joshua to go right while he headed left.

Once again, Jayla dropped to her knees beside her brother and held her breath as the pair moved forward.

Joshua lifted his weapon higher. "Police. Stand down."

So much for stealth mode.

A figure skulked from one tree to another. The suspect's white gear kept them camouflaged in the snowstorm. If she hadn't been looking in that exact location, she would have missed his movement.

"Joshua, to your left!" Jayla yelled.

He pursued the suspect.

Seconds later, an engine roared to life, and a snowmobile bolted from its hidden position, racing across the pass.

Dana crouched low and advanced toward Jayla. "You okay?"

"Yes. Don't let him get away!" She pointed toward the fleeing suspect.

Dana nodded and jumped on the snowmobile, bringing it to life. She zipped after the assailant.

Joshua reached his machine and followed.

"Bryson, we need to get Dekker off the mountain. The storm has intensified, and I'm scared of more avalanches." The wind softened the desperation in Jayla's voice.

He holstered his gun. "Help me get him on my snowmobile." He pointed. "Grab the backpack."

She noticed it lying in the snow. "That was Ethan's. Did you find his—" She stopped, not wanting to say the word *body* out loud. That would make it real, and she wasn't ready to go there yet.

Even though she knew he was gone.

"No. Just his bag beside another drop in the cave." He grazed her arm. "I'm so sorry."

Jayla suppressed the tears welling, wrenching away from his hold. "I need to get Dekker to a hospital. Let's go." She couldn't deal with the emotion of her fallen boss at this point in time. Plus, being around the man who had failed her in the past brought back feelings she thought she'd suppressed. Even though she sensed a change in the man, she waited for the time when Bryson would fail her again.

Give him credit, Jayla. There was probably a reason he froze. She could almost hear her sister Hazel's voice when they first talked about the accident that caused Julie's paralysis.

Should she give him the benefit of the doubt? Jayla snatched up the bag and slipped her shoulders through the straps. This was not the occasion to ponder her unspoken question. Time to get her brother medical help. If something happened to Dekker, Jayla would never hear the end of it from her father—a man who controlled everyone's lives around him, especially his children's.

It was part of the reason Jayla had gone into the army. To get away from his authoritative demeanor.

But it only thrust her from one tyrannical leader to another, and her military career hadn't ended well. After she'd failed to vet intel, her team was attacked and Michael was captured. It was a mistake that not only continued to plague her with guilt but had also turned her fiancé into someone Jayla didn't recognize—an empty vessel of a man. Ultimately, Michael hung himself after they'd rescued him. Would she ever get over her broken heart?

Bryson's engine roared to life, snapping her back to the

moment. He'd placed her brother in front of him in order to keep a tight hold on the injured Dekker.

Jayla commanded Herc to get on her seat, and she sat behind him, keeping him secure. Jayla started her machine and wiped her goggles to remove the snow blocking her vision. The intensity of the storm had increased, and the blinding white pellets would hamper the trip back. She waved her hand and pointed downward, indicating for Bryson to lead them back to the station.

They raced across the mountainous region as fast as they could with the intensified system obstructing their trip. Twenty minutes later, they rode up to the station and parked beside a waiting ambulance.

The paramedics exited their vehicle and sprinted toward Bryson and Dekker.

Jayla cut her engine and dismounted. "Hercules, come."

The golden retriever hopped down.

Jayla ran over to talk to the paramedics. "My brother was shot in the leg and lost a lot of blood. Please help him."

Bryson dismounted the machine and helped the paramedics place Dekker on a gurney.

Jayla grabbed her brother's hand. "I'm coming with you. I need to make sure you're okay." A tear threatened to fall, but she willed it away.

"No, sis. You have work to do here. I'll be fine." He squeezed her hand before letting it go. "Find out what's going on and stop this maniac."

She bit her lip and nodded.

The female paramedic turned to Jayla. "We'll take good care of him. I promise."

Like Jayla didn't already have enough happening... Now she had to deal with her brother getting shot, too.

Bryson studied Jayla's tortured expression as she watched the ambulance whisk Dekker away. From the look on her face, Bryson determined she longed to go with her brother, but his insistence she stay obviously tormented her. "Jayla, you all right?"

She inhaled a deep breath. "I just hope he's going to be okay."

"He will." Bryson guided her toward the door. "Let's get inside and out of this storm." He noticed the snowmobiles. "Looks like Constables Spokene and Hopkins have returned. Let's find out if they caught the shooter."

She nodded and motioned for Herc to follow.

The trio entered the building.

Shouts sounded, followed by a crash.

Jayla halted. "What's going on?"

Constable Spokene approached. "We caught the suspect just as he made a run for the border. You might want to hear what he has to say before we take him in to custody. I've contacted Sergeant Park." She beckoned them forward. "This way. We have him cuffed in the lunchroom." She stopped. "Oh, my husband didn't find any prints on the rifle you found."

"Figures," Bryson said.

They followed her into the medium-sized room that housed two round tables, a fridge and microwave. A pod-cup coffee maker sat on a counter beside a tray of clean mugs. A television blared in the corner.

Spokene sat beside the prisoner.

Jayla grabbed a remote and powered the TV off. She extracted a ball from a pouch in her waistband and threw it to Hercules, pointing to a doggy mat. "Hercules, stay."

The dog obeyed and chewed contently on his prize for good behavior.

Constable Hopkins leaned against the wall.

Jayla yanked a chair from the other table and positioned herself in front of the prisoner. "What's your name?"

Wiry curls poked out from under the man's tuque. He smirked. "I ain't saying nothin'. I have rights."

Bryson stomped forward and leaned on the counter. "Your 'rights'? You shot at us and wounded a park warden."

The man wiggled the cuffs and spoke to Constable Hopkins, motioning toward Bryson. "Why is he here? He doesn't have jurisdiction."

"The governor of Alaska and premier of Yukon would beg to differ," Jayla said, moving into the man's personal space and tugging off his hat. "They gave our CBM task force jurisdiction to patrol the Ogilwyn Pass. You. Shot. My. Brother. Why?"

"I was only following orders. Nothing personal."

Bryson examined the man's face. He guessed him to be in his late thirties. His yellowed fingers spoke of a nicotine habit, and he reeked of alcohol. The man shouldn't have even been riding, let alone shooting a weapon.

Wait... He knew Bryson's jurisdiction. Bryson leaned forward, clasping his hands in a prayer position. "Tell me how you've discovered who we are and where we're from."

"He knows everything about the CBM members." He snarled before continuing. "I also know all about you, *ex–* Trooper Bryson Clarke. You take any—"

"Let's focus on you, shall we?" Bryson didn't want the team hearing more about the lies Gabby had spread about his supposed bribes. "First, tell us your name."

"John Smith." The man's lips turned into another devious smirk.

Bryson had only been in the room for a few minutes and this man's attitude already grated on his nerves. He resisted the urge to slam his palm on the table. "We'll find out your real name when the constables take you into their station. Why not just be truthful?"

The man looked at the floor, but not before Bryson noted the flash of angst that passed over his face.

He was scared of someone.

Jayla scooted her chair closer. "Who are you afraid of?" She had obviously caught the look, too.

The man's gaze swung to Jayla. "He'll kill me. He has spies everywhere."

What did that mean?

"We'll protect you." Bryson addressed Constable Hopkins. "Right?"

The constable shifted his stance and glanced at Spokene before answering. "Of course. We'll talk to our sergeant."

The man slammed his cuffed hands on the table. "You're not listening. He has spies everywhere, even on the force."

"Impossible," Spokene said. "Our team at the Carimoose Bay station is rock solid."

The prisoner snickered. "Are you sure?"

Jayla stood, placed her hands on the table and leaned closer. "Let's start this conversation over. Tell us your real name. Now."

Her abrasive tone caused Hercules to scramble to her side.

Jayla meant business. No denying that fact.

Not that Bryson blamed her. Her friend and leader had died today.

"John Reese."

Spokene wrote in her notepad. "Where are you from?"

"Doesn't matter. What matters is, you'll never stop him."

Jayla gripped both sides of the table. "Stop who?"

"I'm not saying any more." He switched his gaze from constable to constable.

A light bulb went off in Bryson's mind. John didn't trust the police. Perhaps he'd say more if they questioned him alone. "Constables, can Jayla and I have the room for a minute? Then you can take Mr. Reese into custody."

Hopkins straightened, crossing his arms. "That's not our normal procedure, Clarke."

Jayla raised her hand. "It's okay, Joshua. We only need a few minutes. Please?"

The constable's gaze shifted to Jayla, and his eyes softened, lingering for a moment. "Fine."

Did the man have a crush on the beautiful mountain survivalist?

Bryson didn't blame him. A wave of jealousy prickled his neck. *Don't go there, Bry. Remember what Gabby did to you.* Not that it mattered. No way would Jayla Hoyt ever be interested in the man who had put her friend in a wheelchair.

The constables left the room.

Jayla ruffled her dog's head and pointed to his bed. "Hercules, stay."

He obeyed.

Jayla sat back down. "Okay, tell us what's going on. Who do you keep referring to?"

"I only know him as Murdoc." The man's previously stoic face turned ashen, revealing his fear.

"Why are you so scared of him?" Bryson asked.

"Like I said, he has spies."

"On the police force?" Jayla rubbed her temples.

"Possibly, or on your teams."

Just as Bryson suspected. "Tell us more. Who is Murdoc?"

"No idea. I've never met him." His gaze darted to Hercules and back to them. "They only hired me to fire shots at your team."

"How were you contacted?" Jayla asked.

"Through the dark web."

"And what exactly were your orders? Kill us?" Bryson opened the text app on his cell phone. He wanted to take notes.

"More like, scare you off the mountain." He leaned closer to Jayla. "I didn't mean to shoot your brother. He just jumped into my crosshairs as I fired."

"Well, you're going to pay the price for that mistake. If something happens—" She stopped.

Time for Bryson to take over the conversation and give her a moment to compose herself. "Tell us why you were told to scare us off the mountain."

"The text didn't say."

"'Text'? Where's your cell phone?" Jayla asked.

John shimmied in his chair. "Left coat pocket."

Bryson shot upright, tugged a tissue from a box and carefully removed the phone from the prisoner's pocket before setting it in front of him. "Show us."

John keyed in his password and swiped the screen. "Here it is."

Bryson and Jayla moved closer.

Scare the CBM team off Ogilwyn Peak by any means possible. They're headed there now.

Bryson's muscles tensed. "Jayla, look at the time stamp."

1:15 p.m. Today.

She gasped and leaned back. "That was in between the two attacks. How did they know?"

John banged on the table. "Spies."

Just how far did this Murdoc's network reach?

A question formed in Bryson's mind. "John, did you also shoot at us this morning?"

"No." He picked at his nails.

Evading the question.

Jayla snapped her fingers and eyed Bryson. "Wait. You wounded the suspect." She turned to John. "Show us your shoulder."

"It wasn't me, man." John squirmed. "It was my brother, Don."

Jayla rose slowly, staring at the man. "Don Reese is your brother? I helped train him in avalanche safety a few weeks ago."

"He said you were good."

"But yet he took a job to shoot at us? Where is he now?" Jayla asked. "We'd like to talk to him."

"Disappeared. That's part of the reason I took the job this afternoon. I need to find my brother." He paused. "He's all I got."

Constable Spokene walked into the room. "Time's up. Sorry, but our sergeant is here. We need to take the suspect in now."

Constable Hopkins grabbed John, leading him by the arm. "Prison time for you."

John frantically glanced between Jayla and Bryson. "Don't let them take me. I'm as good as dead. He won't let me live."

"Be quiet," Hopkins said, shoving him toward the door. "Go." The three left.

"What's going on, Bryson?" Jayla asked. "I have a feeling something sinister is happening on our mountains."

"Agreed." Bryson zippered his coat. "Let's talk to your boss."

She nodded, and they exited the building.

Some young adults skied toward the group and collided with the constables. "Sorry, man. Didn't see you," one said.

Another bumped into John. "Sorry, dude." She motioned to the others. "Come on, guys. The last lift is leaving now." She skied toward the mountain.

Seconds later, John Reese gasped for air as he swayed and collapsed to the snowy ground. "Find my brother. He knows—" The man stilled, his lifeless eyes staring directly at Bryson.

John's words hammered through Bryson's mind.

He has spies everywhere.

This hit told Bryson that John Reese was right. Murdoc hid his moles right under their noses.

And somehow, John's brother had answers.

FIVE

The snow–ice mix pelted Jayla's window as dusk fell around her SAR station, bringing with it an elevated guard—not only because of the weather but now with two deaths on this tragic day. John Reese and Ethan Ingersoll had lost their lives because of someone named Murdoc. Questions ricocheted through Jayla's tired mind.

Who was Murdoc? Why target their mountain pass and cause avalanches? If that was indeed his game plan, what could he—or she—possibly gain?

The coroner had retrieved John's body, and Joshua had called in Forensics to examine the scene. Preliminary reports suggested some type of fast-acting poison or drug had killed John. The female skier who'd slammed into him had strangely disappeared, leading them to suspect she was the assassin. Unfortunately, her helmet and goggles prevented them from giving any useful identification.

Seemed Murdoc wanted to eliminate any risk of exposure. Was John right? Had Murdoc infiltrated Carimoose Bay's police department? Jayla hadn't known Dana Spokene for long, but Joshua had been a friend for years.

Bryson was in the lunchroom, making himself a coffee. The ranger hadn't left yet to go back to Alaska.

She still had no word on Dekker's condition, but Jayla needed to let her mother know. Plus, she wanted to hear Erica Hoyt's voice, so she punched in her number.

"Hi, dear. How are you?"

"Mom, it's so good to hear your voice." Jayla failed to keep her tone chipper.

"What's wrong, Jay?"

"I have two pieces of bad news. Mom, Dekker was shot today."

Her mother gasped. "What? Is he—"

"He's okay. I don't have an update yet," Jayla said.

A heavy sigh filtered through the airwaves. "I'm going to catch the next flight out."

"Mom, not yet. He wouldn't even let me go to the hospital. I'll get him to call you later and you two can talk." Jayla fingered the diamond ring hanging on her chain. "I lost Ethan today in an avalanche. I can't believe God has taken another person away from me."

"I'm so sorry about Ethan. From what you tell me, he sounded like an amazing man."

"He was, Mom. The best." She wiped a tear from her cheek. "What did I do to deserve this? It's all my fault."

"Young lady, this is not your fault. I can't tell you why God allows tragedies in our lives, but I know that He's there. Always."

"I can't feel Him anymore, Mom. I'm a terrible Christian." She fought to keep her sobs from surfacing.

"Jay, you're not alone," her mother said. "Every believer goes through similar times in their lives. Reach out to Him, and trust."

Would He listen to Jayla this time? "Thanks, Mom. I always love your encouraging words. I miss you."

"Miss you, too, dear. Just remember—pray and then be still. Let Him guide you."

Jayla smiled. Her mother always had the right words whenever Jayla required motivation. "I love you."

"Love you more." She made a puckered-kiss sound. "Talk to you soon."

"Bye, Mom." Jayla ended the call and tossed her phone on the desk. *God, is Mom right? Are You still there? Show me.*

Ethan's backpack sat beside her. Dare she open it? The pain of his death was still too fresh, but she couldn't resist. She unzipped the top. After rummaging through the bag's contents, she stopped at a creased piece of paper. She dug it out and unfolded it.

TODAY YOU DIE

Jayla sucked in a tattered breath.

Someone had cut out block letters from a magazine and glued them to the page to form the ominous message.

Had Ethan been today's target all along? It was the only answer. Why hadn't he reached out to her? She could have helped. She wiped an escaped tear and bounded out of her chair.

Herc stirred from his sleep on the mat in the corner and rose to his feet at her sudden movement.

"Sorry, bud. Didn't mean to scare you."

Bryson appeared at the entrance, coffee in hand. "What is it, Jayla?"

She stepped around the desk and raised the paper. "I found this in Ethan's bag."

His eyes widened. "We need to get this to Forensics. There might be prints on it."

Stupid! She had contaminated the paper without thinking, but she hadn't expected something like this to be in her leader's bag. "I probably ruined any hopes of that happening." She turned the paper around and read it again. "What if Ethan was today's intended target?"

"I think you may be correct." Bryson took a sip of his coffee.

"It has to be the only explanation."

She yanked the scrunchie from her hair and raked her fingers through the tangles. It had been a long day, and all she wanted to do was veg on her comfy plaid couch with a good book.

However, their day had just taken another disturbing turn. She walked back around the desk and plunked herself down in the chair. "I believe you now. Something strange is going on." She stopped to collect her thoughts but came up empty. "What do we do next, Bryson?"

He rubbed Herc's belly before sitting at the table. "Did you catch what John said before he died?"

"Yes. 'Find my brother. He knows.' What do you think he's referring to?"

"Maybe more about whatever this Murdoc is up to?" Bryson sipped his coffee and checked his watch before bolting out of his chair. "Oh no. I didn't realize the time. I need to call Avery."

"Your niece?" Jayla remembered Bryson talking about the little girl back when they'd worked together.

"Yes. She normally goes to Mom and Dad's after school, and I pick her up about this time."

Jayla pointed to the window. "Have you seen the weather? I don't think you'll be going anywhere, even on your snowmobile."

He let out an elongated, audible breath. "Great. Another thing my father will hold against me."

"Why would he do that? It's not like you control the weather." She shoved her hands into her pockets, perplexed why she was defending the man she didn't trust.

"It's a long story, but my father has never forgiven me for Ellie's death. But to be honest, our relationship has always been strained."

Jayla huffed. "Well, if he's anything like my authoritative dad, I understand. All of my brothers and sisters have issues with Frank Hoyt. Ever since Kyle died, he's changed."

"Kyle?"

The image of her younger brother hanging from a rope in his closet flooded her mind, ushering in a rush of emotions she didn't want to unleash. It would only bring forth more feelings about Michael's suicide—plus the unanswered question still haunting her today. Why had God allowed the two suicides of those she loved in her life? Once again, she fiddled with the chain around her neck, reflecting on her mother's earlier words.

"Jayla, where did you go?"

Bryson's question jolted her back into the room. "Sorry. Kyle was my younger brother, who died years ago."

"I'm so sorry. I know what it's like to lose a sibling. My sister and I were close."

Jayla played at rearranging the pens in the holder. "Why did Ellie leave Avery with you and not your parents?"

"We promised to look after each other's families if we passed." He gazed at the floor. "I just wish for a better relationship with my father. Family is important."

Did she also believe that? She had checked on Dekker earlier and found out the doctors had removed the bullet. He would be fine. The doctor told her that Dekker would call her later, but for now, he was resting.

Enough about family. Time to solve the Murdoc puzzle. "What are you going to do? Stay here tonight?"

He stood and stared out the window. "I should have left hours ago." He turned. "However, too much was happening, and I didn't want to leave without getting answers."

Like they had any of those yet. Only more questions.

"Where will you stay?"

"I'll call around town for a place after I get in touch with Mom." He fished out his cell phone.

"I highly doubt you'll find any vacancies. The Cari-moose Bay Winter Festival is on all week. All hotels and B and Bs are booked."

"Not good." He walked over to the couch on the other side of the room. "Perhaps here?"

As much as Jayla struggled with being close to this man, she didn't want him sleeping on a couch that wouldn't ac-commodate his tall frame. "I'm sure my roommate, Kerry, will be okay if you stay with us. We have a guest room."

"I don't want to intrude."

"I insist. It's the neighborly thing to do. Call your niece and parents. I need to find out from Philip how the other K-9s are doing."

"Thank you." He left the room.

She withdrew her cell phone and hit her coworker's speed dial number.

He picked up on the second ring. "Hey, Jayla. What's happening?"

Bryson's earlier words about not knowing who to trust entered her thoughts. However, Philip Oke was like a brother to her, and she wanted to check on Moose and Stella. "How are the kids?"

Their reference for their K-9s.

"Agitated. It's like they sense something's happening." Philip sighed. "Tell me what's going on, Jayla."

Stick with the facts. A phrase Ethan always said to her. "Not entirely sure. Someone shot at our team today, our K-9s' building was destroyed and the suspect the consta-bles detained was taken out right in front of me."

"I'm so sorry you had to go through that—but why do I get the impression you're leaving something out of your story?"

Her eyes shifted to the threatening letter sitting on the

table. For now, she'd keep it confidential. "That's everything for today."

"Fine. Keep your secrets. Please tell me how I can help."

"Just keep Moose and Stella safe. The attack on their building has me stressed." She gripped her phone tighter. "Who would want to kill dogs?"

"Right? It doesn't make sense. Unless they're trying to stop them from doing their jobs." A bark sounded in the background. "The kids are restless. Time for a walk."

"Stay safe, Phil. It's nasty out there. Are you coming in tomorrow?"

"No, I'm taking the dogs on a special mission."

Jayla's suspicion barometer rose. "What are you talking about?" Sergeant Park hadn't shared anything with her about a supposed mission.

"You don't need to know everything that happens at our station." He clicked off.

A chill snaked up Jayla's spine, bringing with it an apprehensive wave.

Another question to add to their growing list in their mysterious situation.

"Dad, I can't help the weather." Bryson clutched his wavy hair, as if that would remove the frustration seeping into his bones. He had hoped his mother would have answered his call, but apparently, Dr. Shannon Clarke was on assignment, inspecting a rock formation found in the Ogilwyn Mountain Pass. His geologist mom consulted frequently. Bryson was proud of her, and their relationship was rock solid. Too bad he couldn't say the same for his father.

"Son, why did you delay your trip? You of all people should have watched the weather pattern and come back when the system picked up. Avery's counting on you."

Are you sure that's the reason you're reaming me out right now, Dad? His father still blamed Bryson for Ellie's death. He claimed that if Bryson hadn't gone fishing early that morning, he could have stopped the grizzly attack and not put Ellie in the position of having to save her daughter's life. Did his father not realize Bryson also struggled every day with the guilt over his sister's death? So many *what-if*s had run through his mind after that day—and still continued to plague him.

Right now, he must deal with solving the mystery of Ogilwyn Mountain Pass.

"I'm working on an important case, and several situations have come up late this afternoon." He wanted to add that his job as a law enforcement park ranger was an important one, but his father had also not forgiven him for giving up his job as a state trooper four years ago. Did Lieutenant Trent Clarke even believe in his son's innocence, even though he'd aided in getting Bryson exonerated after Gabby's foolish allegations?

A black mark had loomed over Bryson's head as he tried to work alongside his fellow state troopers. Unfortunately, most had treated him differently after that, so he decided to train to be a park ranger since he met the qualifications from his previous education and served time in a natural resource technician role. His first love had always been the forest and mountain regions. Plus, his law enforcement background gave him an added bonus. The perfect fit. However, in his father's eyes... Bryson had run away.

Again.

Dad, when will I ever live up to your standards?

"Are you looking into your conspiracy theory again?" his father asked.

Bryson gritted his teeth and counted to ten slowly in his head. He didn't need this agony on top of being shot at twice and climbing an ice wall. "Dad, it's been a rough day, and more evidence has suggested my theory is true."

"What evidence?"

Bryson examined the room. Did the walls have proverbial ears? He must be careful of what he said just in case Murdoc had bugged the station. How else would he have known they had headed back to Ogilwyn Peak?

"I can't explain now." How will his father take his next news? Bryson inhaled deeply before proceeding. "Dad, I need to stay overnight. It's not safe to travel right now. Can Avery stay with you and Mom? I'll be back as soon as I can tomorrow."

Lieutenant Clarke didn't curb his heavy exhale.

Really? Was it that hard of a question? For your granddaughter?

"You know Avery would love a sleepover with Gramma," Bryson added.

"Of course Sweet Pea can stay here." The tough grandfather's tone softened.

"Thanks. Can you put her on the phone so I can explain and say good-night?"

Muffles transmitted in the background. "Hi, Uncle Bry. When are you coming to pick me up?"

Bryson's shoulders loosened at the sound of his precious niece's voice. "Hey, Squirt. How was school today?" Hopefully, he could ease into his bad news.

"Fun. I beat Oliver in the spelling bee match." She snickered. "He stuck his tongue out at me, though."

Bryson suppressed a chuckle. He wouldn't encourage any competitions. "I'm so proud you did well. All of our studying paid off." He walked to the window and observed the continuous snowfall. "Squirt, I have to stay overnight here in Canada. How about a pajama party with Gramps and Gramma?"

"Do you think they'll let me watch a movie?"

See, Dad? Avery doesn't care. It's only you who has the problem.

Wow. He needed to curb his poor attitude, but sometimes his father made it hard. "I'm sure Gramma will let you. Maybe she'll even make popcorn."

"Yippee!"

He smiled at his niece's excitement. "Okay, I gotta run. I love you to the moon and back."

"I love you more. 'Night."

"Let me talk to Gramps again. G'night, Squirt."

"Gramps!" Avery yelled. "Phone's for you."

Bryson sat back down and waited for more ridicule from Lieutenant Clarke.

"Son, don't mess up *this* job." His father's tone bellowed with irritation.

Where did that come from? "Dad, you know I never took a bribe. Gabby lied and trumped up her supposed evidence."

"I know that, but you shouldn't have left the troopers."

Not this argument again. Bryson squeezed the bridge of his nose. "Dad, I'm tired and I don't want to go through this debate all over. I'm doing what I love now."

"Fine. Just be careful of accusing anyone if you don't have evidence."

"I wouldn't do that." How many times would he have to prove himself to this man and make up for past mistakes?

"Gotta go. Get yourself back here pronto tomorrow." He hung up.

Bryson tossed his phone on the table. He'd received the same message from both his father and his boss. "Ugh!"

"Everything okay?" Jayla asked.

He turned at the sound of her voice. He hadn't heard her approach.

She stood in the doorway, leaning against the frame, looking beautiful even at the end of a tiresome and grueling day. He'd always admired her exquisite features—jet-black shoulder-length hair, dark brown eyes and a petite figure. The words *small but mighty* came to mind. Her feistiness was clear, and from what he'd seen, her coworkers dared not cross the mountain-survival specialist.

He was the only one who had—and he'd paid the price.

He shrugged off his reemerging attraction and shoved his hands into his pockets. "Just my father chastising me. Again."

"You ready to leave? My SUV is out back. We can drop the note off with Forensics and then stop at the store for any supplies you need."

"Sounds good." He gathered his phone and coat. "Let's go."

After dropping off the note from Ethan's backpack to Forensics, getting provisions and fighting the slippery roads, Bryson observed Jayla's home as she turned her vehicle into a long driveway. Her bungalow stood at a distance from the street, sheltered by snow-covered trees.

Lights illuminating the building revealed to Bryson that she'd kept good care of her home. Another trait he admired. "Nice. How long have you lived here?"

"Two years. I bought the home when—" She halted.

Bryson stole a glance at her, studying the stoic expression on her face as she chewed her bottom lip.

Something haunted the beauty. The last time they'd worked together—before the incident—she had shared little about what had brought her back to Canada and her reason for leaving the Canadian army. He knew it wasn't easy to leave the military. There was a process to follow. He'd asked, but she changed the subject.

He placed his hand on her arm. "You okay?"

She shrugged away from his touch and parked in the garage. "Tired and hungry. Kerry promised to make supper." She turned off the ignition. "Let's go." She scrambled from the car. After walking to the back of the vehicle, she released Hercules.

Bryson squeezed his lips together. She still didn't trust him—even after what had happened today. Why had he suspected it would be any different? Hoped, yes—but deep down, he guessed it would take more.

He gathered his belongings and followed them into the house.

"Kerry, we're here." Jayla flipped the hall light on.

A slender, tall blonde appeared around the corner, along with a gray-striped kitten at her heels.

Hercules bounded toward the cat.

The kitten arched its back and hissed.

"Muffins, you know Hercules only wants to play." Kerry scooped up the cat and held out her right hand. "I presume you're Bryson?"

He shook her hand. "Yes. Nice to meet you, Kerry. So sorry for intruding. The storm blindsided me."

And other things, but he'd leave that detail out.

"No problem. Our popular winter festival has brought many tourists. Our casa is your casa—right, Jay?" Kerry lifted her brow, tilting her head.

Was that some sort of secret exchange between roommates? What did it mean?

Jayla jiggled out of her jacket and hung it in a closet. "Of course." She held out her hand. "Coat, please."

He removed his and gave it to her. "Well, I appreciate your generosity." He tickled the cat's forehead. "Muffins is a cutie."

"Kerry is a sucker for strays," Jayla said.

"Found her abandoned out in the cold. Hopefully, she'll

warm up to Hercules here." Kerry let the kitten go, and it scurried into another room. "Supper is ready. Hope you like chicken stew."

"Sounds amazing."

Jayla pointed to a hallway. "Guest room is the second one on the right. Bathroom is across the hall. I'll meet you in the dining room in five minutes."

Bryson rubbed his stomach at the thought of a hot meal after such a long, tiring day in the cold.

A crash jerked Bryson awake. A bark followed. He shot upright and listened to determine what the noise could be.

Whoosh!

Hercules's frantic bark warned of immediate danger.

Not good. Bryson whipped off the plaid comforter, then scooped up his weapon and phone as he raced out of the room.

Flames danced in the living room down the hall, confirming his suspicions.

They were under attack.

And he had to get the girls and animals out before the fire consumed Jayla's home.

SIX

Mumbled barking sounded in the distance, pulling Jayla from an intense nightmare. She was attempting to save Michael from killing himself, and Bryson stood off to the side with his arms crossed. She had shouted at him to help, but his body was frozen in some sort of trance. Pounding shook her out of her sleep stupor, and she bounded out of bed.

"Jayla!" Bryson yelled. "The house is on fire. Get up."

"Coming!" She slipped on a housecoat, stepped into slippers and yanked open her door. Heat assaulted her, and she stumbled backward.

Bryson grabbed her around the waist. "I've got you," he said. "I called 911, but we need to evacuate."

Jayla shimmied out of his hold and ran to her roommate's door. She pushed it open. "Kerry, fire!" She waited for her friend to respond before turning back to Bryson. "I'll get Herc. Get Kerry out." *Lord, I can't lose my friend. Protect us!*

Jayla coughed. Hard. The smoke was overpowering her small house. They had little time. She drew her housecoat up over her mouth as she sprinted toward Herc, staying low to help her breathe.

Her K-9 barked.

"I'm coming, bud." She willed her weary legs to move faster and turned the corner into the dining room, where she kept his cage. She thudded to the floor and released the latch. "I've got you."

The dog bounded out from his pen, continuing to bark.

"Hercules, come!" She stumbled back into the hall, turning her head to ensure her retriever had followed.

Herc was at her heels.

The two dashed out the front door and stumbled down the steps. Jayla drew in fresh air, approaching Kerry and Bryson. She embraced her friend. "You're safe. I was scared I lost you."

Kerry Park had moved in with Jayla shortly after Michael had taken his own life. They'd been friends since Jayla had relocated to the Yukon to begin her career as a mountain-survival expert. She'd met the dispatcher on her first day of work, and they'd bonded quickly.

Jayla, hoping Michael would recuperate better in the mountains, had enrolled him in a program at a local rehabilitation center, but only a few short weeks after that she'd found him hanging in his bathroom. Another suicide thrust upon her. Her anger and sadness had collided, shoving her into a pit of despair.

That was two years ago, and nightmares about both Michael and Kyle still plagued her. Thankfully, Kerry had suggested she move in with Jayla. She'd been a true lifesaver.

Kerry backed away from their hug but held Jayla at arm's length. "You okay?"

Jayla coughed again. "Yes, just need fresh air." She breathed in and out.

Bryson bent down and ruffled Herc's ears. "Hey, bud. Glad you're okay."

"Wait. Where's Muffins?" Kerry asked.

"I didn't see her anywhere." Jayla gazed at the flames engulfing her home.

"No... We have to save her!" Kerry whimpered and fell to the snowy ground.

Sirens sounded in the distance. Help was on its way.

Bryson raised himself back to his feet. "Where was she last?"

"Sleeping with me."

Herc barked and zoomed back toward the house.

"No!" Jayla yelled. "Hercules, stay!"

But the dog didn't listen. Was he on a mission to find Muffins?

Jayla took a step, but Bryson yanked her back. "I'll go. You stay here."

He charged into the house.

Lord, protect them. Please listen to me this time.

Jayla held her breath as she hugged her friend.

Moments that seemed like an eternity had passed before Herc trotted back down the steps. Bryson followed, holding the kitten.

He approached them. "Hercules led me right to her."

Jayla slapped his chest. "Do you know how stupid it was to run back into a fire?"

"I wasn't about to let anything happen to both your dog and cat." He shrugged. "What can I say? I'm a sucker for animals, especially cats." He kissed Muffins's forehead before handing her to Kerry.

Jayla resisted the urge to hug Bryson for his bravery. He just gained another notch in her imaginary respect meter. However, she wouldn't let him know that. Yet.

She dropped to her knees and hugged Herc. "You scared me, bud. Don't do that again."

Ruff! Herc licked her face before snuggling deeper into her hug.

Thank You, Lord, for saving us.

Sirens pierced the night as flashing lights appeared

down the road. A fire truck, police cruiser and ambulance approached at lightning speed, stopping at the curb. Firefighters hopped down from their truck and hooked up their hoses.

Dana approached. "What happened? You guys okay?"

"Better, now that we're all out," Jayla said, turning to Bryson. "You were the first to respond. What do you think happened?"

"A crash woke me, followed by a whoosh." Bryson rubbed the stubble on his chin. "I'm guessing Molotov cocktail."

Kerry cringed. "Someone did this on purpose?"

Dana raised her hands. "Let's not jump to conclusions. We'll wait to hear what the fire chief says and go from there." She waved the paramedics over. "Let them check you out. I'm going to talk to the firefighters."

After getting cleared by the paramedics, the group drove to Sergeant Park's residence. Kerry's father had offered his home as a refuge. Jayla was now tucked into bed, staring at the ceiling. No way she'd be able to sleep, as questions clouded her mind. Who had started the fire? Were they targeting Jayla and Bryson because of today?

She balled the comforter into her hands, gripping tightly. The firefighters had stated her home was badly damaged; but thankfully, Bryson's keen ears and quick movements had saved it. They'd also agreed with Bryson's assessment, as they found shattered glass, indicating the use of a Molotov cocktail.

This was a deliberate attack on them.

Lord, please help us find who did this before more lives are taken. For Ethan's sake. I will locate him and find out who did this.

She promised herself she'd do that, but a question emerged.

How, when they had no leads?

* * *

Bryson shuffled toward the kitchen of the log cabin–style home, the coffee and breakfast smells luring him like a fish to bait. He'd finally succumbed to a restless sleep after an eventful night. It was already midmorning. A slow start to the day. Why hadn't anyone awakened him? His weary body required a caffeine jolt, or he'd never be able to function. He walked to the kitchen entryway and stopped.

Sergeant Park hung his head as he prayed out loud.

Prayer… Something his mother had encouraged Bryson to start. However, it was hard after years of being an agnostic. His mother had said God had changed her in an instant and that He'd do the same thing for him. He just had to confess and believe.

His father didn't agree. The man wouldn't budge.

Bryson struggled between their two worlds. One of belief in a loving God, one that wouldn't commit to acknowledging the existence or nonexistence of a higher power.

Approaching footsteps startled him, and he knocked into a nearby chair, exposing his presence to the praying man.

"Sorry. Didn't mean to scare you," Jayla said.

Bryson turned at the sound of her voice as she wiped her eyes and yawned.

Did she realize how cute she looked early in the morning?

I could get used to seeing her pretty face every day.

Where did that thought come from?

He cleared his throat and walked into the kitchen. "It's okay. I need some java."

"Cups are in the cupboard to the right of the sink," Sergeant Park said. "Breakfast is on the stove. Jayla, I'm praying your home will be salvageable."

"Thank you. That means a lot to me." Jayla meandered into the room with Hercules and Muffins at her heels.

Had the animals bonded overnight? Bryson suppressed a chuckle. Maybe the cat knew it had been Hercules that led Bryson to her, saving the little one's life.

Bryson pulled out a cup and turned to the sergeant. "Sorry for interrupting." He filled the mug with coffee, then added cream and sugar.

"No problem," Sergeant Park said. "I frequently pray over our town and residents. Join me."

"I'm good, thanks." Bryson took a sip of coffee, letting the strong roast linger on his tongue for an extra boost.

"You don't believe?" the man asked.

Bryson picked up a plate and added scrambled eggs to it. "To be honest, I'm not sure what to believe. I was raised agnostic, but my mother recently started going to church. She's been trying to convert me."

Jayla slipped beside him and filled a mug with coffee.

Her lavender scent tickled his nose. He breathed in deeper, savoring her presence. What would it be like to have her in his life along with Avery?

"Bryson, did you hear me?" Jayla dished eggs onto a plate.

Busted. Get it together, Bry. Stop fantasizing about something that would never happen. She hates you, re-member?

"Sorry, what did you say?" He moved to the table.

She followed. "I was asking about your father. Is he a Christian?"

Bryson huffed—a little too loudly.

Sergeant Park's eyebrow lifted.

Oops. "Sorry. No. He's on the other end of the spectrum."

"And you're somewhere in between?" The sergeant handed Bryson the napkin holder.

"Something like that." Bryson stuck his fork into the eggs, ready to take a bite, but stopped. "You okay if I eat?"

Jayla sat beside him as Kerry entered the room.

"We say grace in this house," Kerry said. "Let me grab some breakfast, and I'll join you."

Bryson put his fork down and waited for Kerry.

Finally, she sat and caught Jayla's hand and her father's. "We also hold hands during prayer."

Jayla held out her hand. "Come on, Bryson. We don't bite." She snickered.

A noise he loved.

"Fine." He squeezed her hand and bowed his head.

Kerry said grace and asked for protection over the town. "In Jesus's name, amen."

"Amen," her father added.

Jayla remained silent before stuffing eggs into her mouth.

Did she not have the same faith as her friends did?

He set the question aside and picked up his fork.

"Jayla, we found out an extremely high dose of fentanyl killed John, and no prints were on the note you dropped off. Forensics looked at it right away." Sergeant Park sipped on his coffee. "Also, the fire chief confirmed your kennel was destroyed by a pipe bomb."

Jayla dropped her fork. "Wouldn't someone have seen them plant it?"

"I'm sending Constable Hopkins to look through the security footage today. Can you give him access?"

"Of course."

The man stood. "Thanks, Jayla." He kissed Kerry's head. "See you later, pumpkin." He left.

Bryson wiped his mouth with his napkin. "We best get going, Jayla."

Thirty minutes later, Bryson followed Hercules and Jayla to the station.

Jayla stopped.

A crew had removed the rubble from where the kennel had once sat.

She sighed heavily and headed toward the building. "Quick, I want to check the footage before Joshua arrives. Something's not right here. Let's go to the security office."

Good girl. He did too. Bryson opened the front door for Jayla and they stepped inside.

He followed her into the security office, with Hercules close behind.

Jayla pointed to the room's corner. "Hercules, stay."

The dog obeyed and curled up, laying his head on his paws.

"How long have you been Hercules's handler?"

"Two years." Jayla hauled a chair beside her at the security desk. "We'll look at this together. I know your former police experience will help identify things I might miss."

He sat. "Have you and Hercules always had this incredible bond?"

"No." Jayla wiggled the mouse, bringing the computer to life. "I got him just after someone important to me passed away, and I struggled with getting too close. Scared I'd lose—" She stopped.

He placed his hand over hers. "I get it. You didn't want to lose anyone else in your life. Tell me what happened."

She jerked her hand away. "I'd rather not. We have work to do."

He slouched back. "You know you can trust me, Jayla. I've changed since we last worked together."

"Let's not talk about this now." She ran her index finger down a series of electronic files. "Here's yesterday's." She double-clicked on the video.

The footage displayed on the screen.

"What do you think we'll find?" He leaned closer for a better view, trying hard to ignore the woman beside him.

The screen displayed four different camera angles.

She pointed at one. "This is the outside camera, near the kennels. Let's see what happens."

"Fast-forward through it."

She hit the button, and the footage zipped by.

"Wait. Stop there." Bryson pointed.

She obeyed and paused the frame.

They both inched forward, bumping heads and locking gazes.

A strand of hair escaped her ponytail, and he resisted the urge to tuck it behind her ear.

She cleared her throat and gazed back at the screen.

Had she felt the connection too? Images of Gabby floated in his mind, and he concentrated on the computer. No time for useless dreams. Gabby had severed any hopes of him getting into another relationship.

He pointed once more. "Who's that?"

A hooded person stood by the building's corner.

"I'm not sure. Let's keep going." She pressed Play.

The figure turned, revealing the black balaclava concealing their face. The person glanced in all directions before pulling out a metal object and rushing into the kennels. Within minutes, the suspect emerged and ran out of the camera's frame.

Seconds later, the building exploded.

Jayla sucked in a breath and pounded the desk. "I can't believe they tried to kill our dogs. Who would do such a thing?"

"Rewind. I want to get a better look at the figure."

Jayla obeyed and froze the frame as the suspect turned to glance at the camera.

Bryson grimaced. "They knew the camera locations. Coincidence? Or is this person associated with your unit?"

"No one on my team would try to take out our dogs."

Bryson tapped the screen. "Based on this person's stance, it could be a woman."

"Or a smaller male." Jayla slouched back in her chair. Was Murdoc male or female?

"What are you two doing?" Constable Joshua Hopkins walked into the office. "Are you tampering with a police investigation?"

His harsh tone told Bryson he wasn't happy to see them viewing the footage. Why?

Bryson remembered the man's story on the mountain, about how Ethan had supposedly pushed him out of the avalanche's path.

Could it have been the other way around?

SEVEN

Jayla closed the footage and sprang upright. How dare this constable tell her she couldn't view the video feed from her SAR station. She had every right—and why the sudden change in the normally kind constable? She fisted her hands, placing them on her hips. "Joshua, I'm the acting leader here at Carimoose Bay's CBM unit. It was necessary for me to see the footage to get answers about what's happening here. Something is not right."

"Well, from now on, leave the investigation to us." Joshua stepped up to the security desk, invading her personal space. "Or I will take measures to block your leadership."

"Wait a minute," Bryson said. "No one is impeding your investigation."

Joshua waggled his finger at the park ranger. "You need to go back to Alaska, or I will put in a formal complaint to your leader."

Jayla's jaw dropped. "What's going on with you, Josh? You're acting like someone with a chip on their shoulder. Are you trying to be a superhero or something? Come in and save the day?"

Herc jumped to his feet at the sound of Jayla's raised voice. She turned to her dog. "Stay."

He obeyed.

The constable clamped his mouth shut.

Bryson tapped his thumb on the armrest. "Or did you

tell us the truth yesterday about what happened on the mountain? Did you push Ethan toward the avalanche?"

Jayla's gaze snapped to Bryson's. Did he think Joshua had lied? Could he have been responsible for Ethan's death?

The constable pointed to the computer. "Email me the video footage. If I don't get it within the next thirty minutes, I'll be back." He stormed out of the room.

"He never answered your question." Jayla plunked back down in the chair. "Do you really feel he killed Ethan? He's a police officer."

"I'm the last person to cast blame without evidence, but I just feel like something's off."

She chewed her lip as she emailed Joshua the footage.

"It's going to be okay." Bryson sat and gathered her hands in his. "Jayla, did you see what happened on the mountain? Is he capable of something like this?"

She focused on their hands, liking how his encompassed hers. Perfect fit. Heat flushed her cheeks. Bryson's powerful presence played on her mind. She had to admit, the handsome ranger piqued her interest, but his failure in Julie's attack still haunted her. Could she ever forgive and move past that? *Jayla, what are you thinking?* She withdrew from his touch—anything to distance herself from her sudden shift in feelings toward him.

The hurt from Michael's loss invaded her mind, and she resisted twirling the engagement ring hanging around her neck. No way would she open her heart again.

She got up and paced the room, concentrating on yesterday's avalanche event. "I'm pretty sure I remember seeing Ethan push Josh out of the way—but really, the snow obstructed my view. Anything's possible." She threw her hands in the air. "I just don't know."

"It's okay. We'll figure it out." He tapped his thumb on the desk. "I want to put all the information we found on the other avalanches together before I head back to Alaska."

"When will you leave?" Suddenly, the idea of him going back to his side of the border saddened her. *Get a grip, Jayla.*

"Soon, before my leader has my head. He's already got me on probation because I questioned the avalanche reports."

Jayla's cell phone buzzed, and she fished it out of her pocket, checking the screen. Her brother. "It's Dekker. I gotta take this. Don't leave without saying goodbye."

She hit Accept and walked out of the room. "Dekker, how are you?"

Herc's claws clicked on the floor behind her, indicating he'd followed her into the hallway.

"Tired and groggy, but alive." Dekker's faint voice revealed his condition. "I wanted to touch base and let you know I'm going to be just fine."

"It's good to hear your voice. When I saw you get shot, I was so scared." Her voice quivered. "I know we haven't spoken lately and I'm sorry for that." Guilt plagued Jayla at cutting off communication with her brother.

"Sis, it's a two-way street. I haven't tried to call you either. After I caught wind of something happening in your region, I had to come."

Jayla gripped the phone tighter. "I'm sorry for not being a good sister. Can you forgive me?"

"As long as you can do the same for me."

She chuckled. "Of course. Hey, Mom wants to come visit. You might want to give her a call to let her know you're okay."

"She can come as long as she leaves Dad home. You know how he can be."

Yes, she did. All too well.

A commotion sounded through the phone. "Jay, I gotta run. Nurses want to check my incision. Let's get together once everything settles down."

"Sounds good. Get better soon. Love you."

"You too. Bye."

She stuffed her phone back into her pocket. *Lord, help him be okay.*

Thundering footfalls approached from the hall.

Jayla pivoted.

Kerry appeared in the doorway. "You're needed. Just got reports of an avalanche and a missing skier." She paused. "Jayla, the skier is Don Reese."

Jayla's heart rate galloped, and she turned to her K-9. "Hercules, come."

They had a search and rescue to conduct, but thoughts nagged in her mind.

Was this avalanche man-made too? And was Don leading them into some sort of trap?

"Jayla needs my help, sir. I can't leave now." Bryson hated the sound of desperation in his voice, but he knew he had to convince Supervisor Leon Thamesford the value he brought to the Canadian team. News of another avalanche and missing skier propelled him to a heightened guard. It was necessary for Bryson to determine whether Murdoc had orchestrated this newest event. However, he kept that information from his leader until they could gather more evidence.

"Don't they have others to help?"

The man's tone told Bryson he was on shaky ground. If they couldn't prove his theory soon, would Bryson still have a job?

If not, he'd never hear the end of it from his father.

Bryson chose his words carefully. "Jayla specifically asked for me to stay and help. With Ethan's death, they're a man down. Please, sir. I'll be back by the end of the day." *I hope.*

Although, the idea of leaving Jayla brought a wave of

sadness. Being in her company had given him a spark of joy. Something he missed in his life. Well, not that Avery didn't bring him happiness, but—

Stop right there, Bry. Don't even go there. Avery doesn't need another broken relationship.

Avery had mourned Gabby's absence after the breakup, even though Bryson knew she'd get over it quickly. It wasn't like the woman had paid that much attention to his niece, but Avery had enjoyed having another female around once in a while.

"Fine. I best see your hide tomorrow morning, or there will be consequences." Thamesford clicked off.

Bryson wiped the perspiration from his forehead and walked back into Jayla's office. "I'm good to stay. Well, my boss wasn't happy, but he approved it."

"Good." Jayla grabbed a tablet and clicked on its keyboard, and a map popped up on the wall monitor. She walked over to the screen. "Here's what we know."

Bryson reviewed the diagram.

Jayla pointed. "This is where the avalanche was reported. This may have been an accident. We don't know for sure someone triggered an explosion."

"Agreed, but let's keep an open mind. I want to see the area for myself."

"Well, that's the issue." She enhanced the picture. She pointed to a stretch on the screen. "This is where the avalanche happened, and Don's last beacon reading was Brookfox Ridge."

Bryson whistled. "That ridge stretches along Brookfox Mountain from the Yukon into Alaska." Another mountain among Ogilwyn Pass.

"Right, and it's only accessible by helicopter."

Bryson rubbed his chin. "How long has he been missing?"

Jayla clicked on her tablet. "Wife reported he didn't

come home last night. Plus, we know from John that his brother had disappeared."

"Wait… He's been on the ridge all night?" Bryson winced. "This will be a recovery, not a rescue."

A knock sounded at the door. "Not necessarily," a deep voice said.

Bryson turned.

A man dressed in a red SAR flight uniform leaned in the door frame.

"Thank heavens you're here." Jayla gestured toward the man. "Bryson, this is our pilot, Jeff."

Jeff extended his hand. "Call me Too Tall."

Bryson suppressed a chuckle. Jeff's call sign suited him. He towered over Bryson, which made him at least six-four. "Nice to meet you. Why do you think the skier may be alive after all this time, especially after an avalanche?"

"Dispatch has been communicating with him. That's how we knew he was on Brookfox Ridge."

"I'm guessing the avalanche propelled Don onto the ridge?" Jayla asked.

"Correct," Too Tall said. "He got caught in the storm late yesterday and couldn't get off the mountain. The high winds prevented us from getting to him. Don says he trained under you, Jayla, and that saved his life in the avalanche. Time to get him off the mountain."

"Thankfully, the temperatures rose, but that puts the area at greater risk of more avalanches." Jayla collected her coat. "We need to get to him now. Hercules, come."

Five minutes later, after Too Tall had completed his pre-flight checklist, the group—including another SAR member, Isaac Park—lifted off in the helicopter and headed toward Brookfox Ridge. Bryson stared out his window and marveled at the beautiful scenery. He loved winter. The snowcapped mountains and wilderness created a gorgeous white canvas. The sight made him think a master

creator did indeed exist. His mother would tell him God
had painted the landscape. Could he also believe that? He
wanted to. Ever since Ellie's death, he had questioned everything, including his father's way of thinking. Maybe
his mother had it right. God did exist and loved them all
unconditionally.

Was that really possible?

Movement from a distant mountain caught his attention. He pulled out his binoculars and peered through them.
Snow collapsed, plummeting at lightning speed down the
slope. "Avalanche!" He pointed.

Jayla snatched the binoculars. "That's Brookfox Ridge.
Don's been buried again." She tapped on the seat. "Jeff,
we need to get there now!"

Too Tall banked left and radioed their location to Dispatch. "ETA, two minutes. We can't get to the ridge, so
we'll land close to the site and then take you up via longline."

Bryson studied Jayla's face.

Her eyes widened, and she averted her gaze to Hercules.

"Jayla, have you attempted a longline rescue before?"
Bryson feared her answer. Longlining was not a simple
task and not done frequently.

She looked back at him, inhaling and exhaling heavily.
"No. It's rarely used, but we've trained for it multiple times."

Two minutes later, they scrambled out of the helicopter,
and Isaac handed Jayla a hook attached to a line. "This is
a two-hundred-foot-long rope. Do you have the extended
leash?"

"Yes." She fastened the hook to the K-9's harness. "Here
we go, bud. We can do this."

Hercules barked.

Too Tall's radio crackled.

"Team, be advised a storm is approaching quickly,"

Kerry said. "You don't have much of a window here. Meteorologists are calling it a tsunami of snowstorms."

"Copy that." Too Tall pointed back to the helicopter. "Hurry, we need to get Hercules to that ridge."

Bryson's muscles locked.

Great. A risky rescue and a multitude of impending storms.

Not a good combination.

Jayla prayed a silent, desperate prayer as she hooked herself up to the rope with Herc, tethering them together tightly. *Lord, please hear me. Keep us safe, and help us find Don fast. I'm counting on You.* She kissed her dog's forehead and held his face in her hands. "Herc, we can do this. Remember our training."

Ruff! He snuggled into her touch.

Was her dog sensing her wave of trepidation? *Breathe, Jayla. Breathe. Show Herc you're stronger than you feel.*

"Jayla, you ready for liftoff?" Jeff yelled from inside the helicopter.

Not really. She counted to five slowly in her head, willing her thudding heartbeat to go back to normal. *You've trained for this.* Still, training and actually doing a risky longline rescue live were two different things entirely.

She hugged Herc tightly and bowed her head. "Keep us safe, Lord."

"Amen." Bryson squeezed her shoulder. "I'll be guiding you over coms." He jumped into the chopper.

She tightened her helmet and adjusted her goggles, then secured her grip on Herc. She gave Jeff a thumbs-up.

The helicopter lifted into the air and moments later, she and Herc were hoisted upward, rising up and over the mountains as they traveled toward the ridge. A wave of angst skittered through her body, but she inhaled and caught sight of the peaks. The breathtaking beauty stunned her every time. *This never gets old.*

She noted the approaching darkened clouds. They only had one shot at this rescue before the weather turned ugly.

Lord, lead Herc to Don.

Not only did Jayla want to save the man's life, but they also required answers from him on Murdoc's operation.

She pushed out the breath she'd been holding and scanned the ridge. *Almost there, bud.*

"Approaching the site, Jayla," Bryson said through their coms. "You've got this."

The helicopter eased into position as it hovered over the ridge until Jayla's feet plunged into the snow and she yanked on the rope to give them slack. After unharnessing Herc, she dropped him into the snow and tethered his 115-foot leash to the gear. She would not lose her dog.

She squatted to be at eye level with her retriever to ensure he'd hear her command. "Hercules, search!"

He moved swiftly through the snow along the long, wide ledge, working in a triangle pattern side to side. He stopped to sniff at various points.

Jayla prayed his scent cone would work fast. He had to hurry before the wind increased. "Come on, boy. Find Don quickly. We need to get off this mountain."

She also knew it had been a few minutes since the last avalanche had pounded on top of the man. Would he remember everything she'd taught him? Being buried under a ton of snow messes with the mind, and all instructions could be wiped from memory. The key was to remain as calm as possible.

"Come on, Herc! Find him." Jayla walked in the direction her retriever had gone.

"Anything?" Bryson asked via her headset.

"Not yet. He's—" She stopped and listened.

A muffled bark sounded nearby.

"I think he's found something. Just a sec." Jayla tugged for more slack and inched along the ridge.

Herc's head was buried in the snow as he dug ferociously, tail helicopter-wagging.

"He's found something. I need to help dig." Jayla raced to Herc's side. She took out her shovel and dug in a paddle motion.

Within minutes, they reached Don.

Jayla tunneled the snow out around him. "Can you hear me?"

Don's face appeared, and he gasped for air.

"He's alive!" Jayla continued to dig until she could pull him out of the snow. "You okay, Don?"

He clutched his shoulder and gulped in breaths. "You saved me even after I shot at you. Why?"

"We can talk about it later. We want answers—but for now, we need to get to safety." Jayla rubbed Herc's back. "Good boy."

He barked.

Jayla stood and spoke into her coms. "Hooking us back up. Stay tuned."

"Hurry, Jayla." Jeff's heightened tone revealed anxiety. "Storm is almost here."

After attaching Don to a harness, she hooked the trio together and jerked the rappel line. "Ready. Up."

The line went taut and the three were lifted into the air, slowly rising over the mountaintops before they reached their landing site. The crew then unhooked them and helped the injured Don into the helicopter.

"He needs medical attention—fast," Isaac said into his radio.

Once again, the chopper lifted to return to their station.

Bryson embraced Jayla. "You were awesome. So glad you're safe."

His hug enveloped her body, giving her a rush of peace

after a stressful situation. *I could get used to his arms around me.*

Herc nudged into their hold, breaking them apart and tearing her from thoughts of the handsome, rugged park ranger.

Bryson laughed and tousled Herc's ears. "You were awesome, too, Hercules."

Jayla fished out his toy and gave it to the dog. "Your reward is well deserved, my friend. When we get back, I'll give you your favorite special treat."

Ruff!

Jayla giggled at his mumbled bark as he chewed on his toy.

"Um… We have a problem," Jeff said through the headset.

Jayla tensed. "What?"

"Weather at our station has turned nasty. We need to travel in the opposite direction."

"Head to our station at Faircord Junction," Bryson said. "We have a medic to tend to Don's shoulder. I'll contact my leader."

"Copy that." Jeff banked the helicopter again and proceeded to the Alaska border.

Jayla leaned back as Bryson spoke into the radio, clearing their landing with his team and requesting Chris meet them on the helicopter pad.

They were almost to safety.

Thank You, Lord.

Fifteen minutes later, Jayla turned her head to view the mountainside terrain as they neared the border.

"Starting our descent," Jeff said.

The mountain wilderness crept up quickly as they lowered in altitude. Jayla noted a clearing off to the left where they'd land. It grew in size as they approached.

A stream of light appeared to the right.

She popped up.

Jayla knew what was hurtling upward in their direction at lightning speed. "RPG! Bank left. Now!"

The helicopter leaned sharply, jostling her toward Bryson.

She held her breath, praying the rocket-propelled grenade would miss its target.

A tail strike spun the helicopter.

"Crash position!" Jeff yelled. "Compensating."

The chopper righted itself, bringing it out of the spin as Jeff fought to keep them in the air. However, the grenade had done its damage, and they hit treetops on their way to the ground.

"Mayday, Mayday, Mayday. Faircord Junction Station, this is CBM Canadian squad Chopper 3, declaring an emergency. RPG hit to our tail. Going down one mile northeast of your—" Jeff's plea broke as they crashed through the treetops.

Jayla hugged Herc and assumed a crash position.

Lord, protect us.

Seconds later, the chopper thudded into the snowy ground.

Jayla's head crashed into the window, hurtling her into darkness.

EIGHT

Bryson woke with a start, trying to recollect where he was and what had happened, but his foggy brain wouldn't focus. A distant bark jerked him fully awake. Right, the crash. A smoky hue filled the helicopter's interior as fuel assaulted his nose. He bolted upright. They had to escape before the chopper exploded. Spots obstructed his vision as a plague of dizziness from his sudden movement overtook him. He rubbed his temples to clear the wave and focused his attention on an unconscious Jayla.

Hercules lay nestled in the hold she'd obviously latched onto before they crashed. The dog licked her face.

He was trying to wake his handler.

Bryson reached over and placed his fingers on her neck. Steady rhythm. *Thank you.* He shook her shoulder. "Jayla! Wake up."

Don stirred across from him. "What happened?"

"Crashed." Bryson unbuckled his lap belt and observed the men.

Don sat wide-eyed, a trickle of blood seeping down his face.

Isaac was slumped in his seat.

Bryson felt for a pulse but found none. The man had perished. Remorse for the loss of life bull-rushed Bryson, but he set it aside and concentrated on the others in the chopper. He moved into the cockpit and found a dazed Too Tall. "You okay, buddy?"

The pilot rubbed a gash on his head. "Will be."

Hercules's sudden excessive barking warned Bryson of imminent danger.

The fuel smell overpowered the aircraft as a flame shot up at the chopper's tail.

"Time to get out. It's gonna blow." Bryson unbuckled the man. "You okay to move?"

"Yes. I'll go around back and help evacuate." He pushed the door open and fell out into the snowy wilderness.

Bryson scrambled back into the rear.

Too Tall appeared at the door and yanked it open, beckoning them forward. "Come on."

Don unbuckled himself and stumbled through the opening.

Too Tall climbed into the chopper, checked Isaac's pulse, and sighed before lifting the man's body. "We don't leave our men behind."

"Understood." Bryson stole another glimpse at the rear. Flames continued to rise, reminding him he only had seconds. He unsnapped Jayla's buckle and unhooked Hercules. "Hercules, go!"

The dog whined and licked Jayla's face again.

Hercules was scared for his handler.

"I've got her, bud." Bryson lifted Jayla and tightened his hold on her, turning to the dog. "Hercules, come."

Bryson stepped over fallen debris and staggered through the escape route.

Hercules hopped out of the helicopter.

Too Tall lifted Isaac over his shoulder. "Run!" The whooshing of the growing fire muffled his cry.

Bryson sprinted.

Hercules barreled past him and turned, barking as if yelling at Bryson to move faster.

Bryson mustered his strength and darted toward the pilot, struggling through the deep snow. Jayla jostled in his arms, but he couldn't help it. He must get away from the blast trajectory—and fast.

Seconds later, the helicopter exploded.

The heat propelled Bryson forward. He stumbled but caught himself.

The group trudged deeper into the trees.

Bryson set Jayla down and leaned her against a fallen trunk.

Too Tall did the same with Isaac before dropping beside Bryson. "That was close."

"Too close." Bryson once again gently shook Jayla. "Come on, wake up." He fingered a bump on her forehead. "She hit her head and needs medical attention."

"What about me? I do, too." Don stumbled to a tree and slouched against it.

"You?" Bryson sprang to his feet and rushed over to the man. He gripped his collar. "If it wasn't for you, we wouldn't be here."

Don's eyes practically bulged. "He made me."

"Let me guess—Murdoc?"

Don nodded.

Bryson poked his finger into the man's chest. "Do you realize your brother is dead? Taken out by an assassin I'm guessing Murdoc sent?"

"Johnny is gone?" the man asked. "When?"

"Yesterday."

Don wrung his gloved hands over and over. "I tried to keep him out of all this."

"Bryson?" Jayla's weakened voice sounded behind him.

He turned and rushed back to her, then dropped to the ground. "You're awake."

Hercules cuddled closer, licking her face.

She smiled. "Love you, too, bud."

"Hercules here has been worried about you." Bryson brushed a strand of hair from her eyes.

"Did he tell you that?" She shifted position and winced.

"He did." Bryson read the painful expression on her

twisted face. Tension knotted his neck muscles at the thought of someone intentionally trying to harm her. "Don't move. Where are you hurt?"

"My head." She rested her head on Hercules, her body trembling. "The others?"

"I'm afraid Isaac didn't make it," Bryson said.

"No!" A tear tumbled down her cheek.

"I'm sorry." Bryson wiped her face. "Did you know him well?"

"He was Kerry's brother. How am I gonna tell her he's gone?"

Too Tall sat opposite her. "He was a good man."

Jayla rested her hand on the pilot's. "Jeff, I'm so glad you're okay. I don't know what I would have done if we lost you, too."

"Why would someone attack my chopper?" Too Tall asked. "It doesn't make sense."

Jayla pointed at Don. "Ask him. I bet he has information about what's been happening in our mountain pass."

Bryson withdrew his radio. "First, we need to get you help." He pressed the button. "Faircord Junction, do you read?"

Silence.

Bryson repeated the process, but no response came. "Too Tall, does your radio work?"

The pilot tried his, but nothing happened.

"It won't be long before the storm hits here, too. We have to either find shelter or make our way to my station." Bryson glanced around, trying to get his bearings. He turned back to Too Tall. "Do you remember exactly where we were when we went down?"

"I was too busy steadying Beulah." He looked over at the wreckage.

"Sorry she's gone," Bryson said.

"Wait. I remember seeing your chopper pad seconds before the RPG hit." Jayla eased herself slowly into a standing position, but she staggered.

Bryson wrapped his arm around her waist. "I've got you. Okay, so if that's the case, we can't be far."

"Which direction should we go?" Too Tall asked.

Bryson shifted and helped Jayla lean against a tree. "I'll be right back."

He trudged through the snowy woods toward the wreckage, wanting to get his bearings. He'd patrolled this wilderness multiple times and knew it like the back of his hand.

Well, that was in the best of times. Not after being attacked and in a chopper crash.

He studied the downed helicopter. A billowing stream of smoke rose higher, creating a beacon. Hopefully, it would help the others find them—but had they heard Too Tall's distress call?

Bryson moved to a break in the trees and determined their location. He dashed back to the group. "Jayla, can you walk?"

"I think so." She rubbed the bump on her head. "I'm a bit dizzy."

"The rest of you okay to walk?" Bryson asked.

The other two men nodded.

"Okay, I figured out our location and know which way we need to walk." He pointed to the chopper. "That smoke should be visible from my station, and hopefully they heard Too Tall's Mayday call. Time to move. Stay close together. Follow me."

Once again, Too Tall lifted Isaac over his shoulder. His intent was clear. He wasn't leaving the man behind, even if it cost him his strength and speed.

Bryson looped his arm through Jayla's. "I've got you."

Strangely, she didn't argue, proving to him she was weaker than she'd let on. *Time to get you to a medic, Jay.*

Had he really just thought of her using her nickname?

* * *

Jayla buried the pain throbbing in her head and resisted the urge to flinch. She wouldn't let on how weak her body really felt after the crash. Her jellylike legs struggled to move, but she willed them forward. A gust of wind sprayed a dust of fresh snow onto her face. She wiped it off and checked the dark cloud–infested sky. Flakes tumbled and increased with every step she took. She prayed the walk wouldn't be long, or else she didn't know if she'd make it to Bryson's station. Thankfully, leaning on his strength helped her move, as it also chipped away at the ice surrounding her heart. Could she have been wrong about the man beside her?

Herc nudged in closer as he walked by her side. Her dog was excellent at sensing his handler's mood. She reached down and stroked his head. *Thank You, Lord, for keeping us safe.* Another tear threatened to fall over the loss of Isaac. How would she break the news to Kerry and her father? They were a close family.

Jayla removed her cell phone. Best get it done. No signal. She'd call later.

"Penny for your thoughts," Bryson whispered close to her ear.

"Just thinking about family." She blew out a sigh and noted her breath lingering in the cold air.

"Are you close to yours?"

"Yes and no. I'm closest to my sister, Hazel. Don't hear from my other siblings very often. Birthdays, Christmas, special occasions." Jayla longed for a big reunion like in the good old days—her family all sitting around her parents' long oak table at the Hoyt Hideaway Ranch—but her father's attitude since Kyle's death had distanced them and added a wedge into their family dynamics. *Maybe one day.*

She snuck a peek at Bryson and admired his stubbled chin. She couldn't deny her attraction to him, but she wondered about his story. Something had tormented him that day when the grizzly appeared. His reaction had been quite clear, and Julie paid the price.

She bit her lip and looked away. "How much longer to your station? What I wouldn't do right now for a steaming cup of hot chocolate with marshmallows and whipped cream on top."

He chuckled. "Sounds divine. We're—"

Multiple engine roars vibrated through the trees.

Jayla drew in a breath. Were the approaching snowmobiles friend or foe?

Bryson stopped and raised his fisted hand.

Their party halted.

"Take cover." Bryson nudged Jayla behind a tree.

Herc and the group followed.

Four snowmobiles approached. One rider wore a jacket with a red vest and white cross on top.

"That's my team." Bryson walked back into the clearing and waved his arms.

They stopped and the riders hopped off, removing their helmets.

Jayla recognized Chris, their medic, and Faith—the ranger with the Bryson-crush.

Why did that now prickle at her? *Get a grip, Jay. They're here to take you to safety.*

Bryson approached the other two individuals. "Supervisor Thamesford, so glad to see you." He gestured toward Jayla. "This is Jayla Hoyt and Hercules."

"It's Leon." The forty-something man held out his hand. "Jayla, I've heard a lot about you and your lifesaving Hercules. Appropriate name, by the way. Ethan spoke highly of you. Sorry for your loss."

"Thank you. Nice to finally meet you, sir." Jayla accepted his handshake. "Hercules is the best of the best."

The dog barked as if in agreement.

The group chuckled.

The fourth member squatted in front of Herc, ruffling his ears. "Herc is a beaut. I'm Tom Rayborn, our station's K-9 handler."

"Yes, we've spoken on the phone. Glad to meet you in person." Jayla pointed to their pilot. "This is Jeff, our chopper pilot. That's Don, our prisoner."

"The one you saved on Brookfox Ridge?" Chris strode toward Don.

"Yes."

"Why is he a prisoner?" Faith asked.

Jayla zippered her coat closer to her neck to block out the biting wind. "Because he shot at us yesterday and has some explaining to do."

Chris lowered his goggles. "There's blood on your jacket, Don."

Don pointed a finger at Bryson. "He shot me."

Chris turned back to Bryson, his eyes narrowing. "Why doesn't that surprise me?"

Jayla didn't miss the animosity toward Bryson. She'd seen it yesterday, too. She put her hands on her hips. "He tried to kill us. Bryson had every right to fire back." Wow… Now she was defending him? Lots had changed since yesterday.

"What caused your chopper to crash?" Leon asked.

Bryson raised his hands. "Can we talk about this at the station? It's cold and we need to all be checked out, including Hercules. Sir, can you arrange for a vet to come?"

"Absolutely. A team is also on their way to the crash site. We'll know more about it later." Leon pointed to his machine. "Jayla, you and Hercules come with me. Bryson, you're with Faith."

Of course he'd pair them together.

Jayla ignored the green envy creeping in and gestured Herc into the snowmobile's rack. "Up."

He hopped inside.

An hour later, after getting checked out by paramedics, Jayla nursed her cup of hot chocolate in the Faircord Junction station's lunchroom. She'd finally spoken to Kerry and told her about the crash. She'd taken the news of her brother's death hard. Jayla had hated to do it over the phone, but she wanted to be the one to tell her.

Jayla rubbed Herc's body. He'd also been examined and fed. She leaned down and kissed his snout. "I'm so glad you're okay, bud. I don't know what I'd do if I lost you."

Herc licked Jayla's face in response.

Images of the RPG flying toward them sent bolts of anger jabbing her body. Why target their team? Had they come too close to finding out the truth?

Bryson sat across from her, writing a report for his supervisor while they waited for word on Don's condition.

A knock sounded, and Leon walked into the room. "How's it going?"

"Finally feeling warm again." Jayla sipped her hot chocolate. "I don't normally mind the cold, but for some reason, it seeped deep into my bones." She pictured herself locked in her mother's restaurant freezer years ago and shuddered at the memory. It had started her fear of enclosed places.

The supervisor plunked down into a chair. "Can we talk about the crash now?"

The wind howled and rattled the window. Jayla got up and peered outside. The storm had intensified, now delaying their trip back to Canada. Would they have to stay the night? She turned to Leon. "Where's Jeff?"

"He went back to the crash site with a team member. Said he wanted a better look. Not that they'll find much in the rubble, though." He tapped his thumb on the desk. "He mentioned an RPG hit you. That true?"

"It is." Bryson put his pen down. "Thankfully, Jayla saw it coming at us, and Too Tall evaded a direct hit."

"I don't understand why your chopper was attacked." Leon leaned back and crossed his arms.

Jayla glared at Bryson, tilting her head and sending him a silent question. Would he understand her look?

Just how much did he want to share with his boss?

Bryson clasped his hands. "Sir, I need to catch you up to speed. Yesterday, we were shot at. Twice."

Leon slammed his hand on the table. "Why am I just hearing about this now?"

Jayla sat back down. "It's been a busy twenty-four hours. Our station's kennel was also bombed."

"Chris told me. Are your dogs okay?"

"Yes. Thankfully, Herc was with me, and the other two were with my coworker." Jayla rubbed Herc's ears. "Our constables caught the man who shot at us while we were trying to locate Ethan's body and…" She couldn't go on. Ethan's death was still too hard to fathom. Had it only been twenty-four hours ago? It seemed like an eternity. "We interrogated the man and found out—"

The door opened, and Chris rushed inside. "Don's been taken to Faircord Junction General Hospital."

The group shot out of their chairs.

"What happened?" Jayla asked.

"He started convulsing," Chris said.

Bryson put on his coat. "We need to get there now."

Her thoughts exactly. They still required answers.

Answers that could hopefully help solve this Murdoc mystery.

Bryson paced the hospital's corridor, waiting for word of Don's condition. Ramsay had insisted they not interrogate him earlier, and now they may have missed their window for getting answers. Bryson banged his fist on his leg. Once again, Ramsay had gotten in the way. Why? Mistrust crawled up his body and settled into his head.

Somehow, Murdoc had eyes everywhere. Did that mean he was well-connected, or did he indeed have spies, like John Reese had alluded to earlier?

Jayla placed her hand on his shoulder. "You okay?"

He jumped at her touch. He hadn't realized she'd gotten up from her chair and approached.

"Sorry. Didn't mean to scare you."

He raked his fingers through his hair. "Not your fault. My nerves are frayed."

"Well, getting shot at twice and surviving a helicopter crash will do that to you."

Hercules nudged his leg.

Did the dog also sense his unraveled anxiousness? *You need to reel it in, Clarke. You're not helping the situation.*

"I'm just frustrated, with too many questions, and I still don't understand why Ramsay wouldn't let us talk to Don earlier. Now it may be too late." He plunked down into a chair in the small waiting room.

Jayla sat. "He probably didn't want to put added stress on Don's injured body. You suspect it's more than that?"

"I don't trust him. Lately, he's been acting differently toward me."

"What do you mean?"

Bryson replayed the past few weeks through his mind, looking for the right words to describe Ramsay's behavior. "Sharp. Condescending. Picking apart all my decisions. That sort of thing."

"Did you get along previously?"

"I thought so. I'm not sure what changed."

Jayla patted Hercules's head. "Maybe he has something going on in his personal life. A breakup. Family issues. That can definitely affect someone's personality."

"You speaking from experience?"

She sat back. "No comment."

Bryson analyzed the woman beside him. *What's your story?*

She caught his gaze, and their eyes locked.

His heart fluttered. What was happening to him? *You can't go there.*

Once again, he stood. Anything to distance himself from his growing feelings.

The hospital emergency doors slid open, and a doctor walked through, lowering his mask as he approached. "Is your name Clarke?"

"Yes, Ranger Bryson Clarke." Bryson pointed to Jayla. "This is Jayla Hoyt. How's Don doing?"

"I can't discuss a patient's case. You're not family, but he's asking to speak with you both." He eyed Hercules. "You can have five minutes, but leave the dog here."

Jayla pointed to his vest. "He's my partner and doesn't leave my side."

Her firm voice revealed she wasn't taking no for an answer. Bryson didn't know the hospital protocol on SAR dogs, but he kept his steady gaze on the doctor, waiting for his answer.

"Fine. Five minutes, then you're outta here." The doc punched in a code and hit the button to open the sliding doors.

The three followed the doctor into the emergency station that housed four beds, each separated by a curtain. He pointed to the last one at the end of the row. "He's in there. I'll be back." He walked toward a nurse.

Bryson opened the draped divider and approached Don's bedside. His shoulder had been bandaged, and an IV was hooked up to his arm. "The doctor said you wanted to see us. How are you doing?"

Don's eyes widened. "I'll live, but I wanted to tell you that I reacted to whatever your medic gave me at the station. Where'd you get that incompetent guy, anyway?"

What had Ramsay given him? More doubts over the medic's behavior filled Bryson's mind.

Jayla inched closer, holding Hercules by his leash. "Tell us about Murdoc. Who is he, and what's his operation?"

Don turned away. "Tell me what happened to Johnny."

"He was targeted outside Jayla's station," Bryson said.

"I tried to keep him out of it." Don's voice quivered.

"What do you mean?" Jayla asked. "What's your connection with this Murdoc?"

"They only hired me to keep people away from certain mountain ranges, Ogilwyn Peak being one of them. I don't know Murdoc or what the operation is."

"What were you doing on Brookfox Ridge?" Bryson wanted to keep him talking before the doctor returned.

"Keeping watch."

Jayla gripped the bed's railing. "Watch on what?"

"To make sure no one came to the ridge. But what I heard almost got me killed."

"What?" Bryson asked.

"I only heard snippets—but something about the area's avalanches of late and dynamite."

Jayla's gaze diverted to Bryson's. Was she thinking the same as him?

That they were correct in being suspicious about the avalanches?

Bryson leaned forward. "Tell us more."

"Only other word I caught was 'copper,' and then they saw me spying. They had the nerve to shoot at me even though I was supposedly working for them. When I ducked for cover, I fell onto the ridge."

"What happened—"

"Time's up. We need to prep him for surgery." Another masked doctor interrupted Bryson's question. He inserted a drug into Don's IV.

Hercules growled.

"What is it, boy?" Jayla asked.

Bryson's mistrust meter spiked. "Surgery for what, Doctor? I thought the bullet grazed him."

"X-ray showed fragments. We want to get them out. Please leave." The man snapped his glove on his wrist before leaving the enclosed bed station.

Bryson turned to Don. "We're not done talking. You take care."

He leaned close to Jayla as they returned to the hallway. "I want to talk to that doctor." He scanned the corridor, but the man had disappeared.

The first doctor spoke to a nurse at the station before turning to them. "Good, you're leaving. Our patient needs rest."

Jayla fisted her hands on her hips. "Wait—weren't you prepping him for surgery for the bullet fragments in his shoulder?"

"What? There are no—"

Warning bells suddenly blared, silencing the doctor.

"Code blue. Bed four!" the nurse yelled into the phone.

The medical team darted toward the last station in Emergency.

Don's bed.

Jayla grabbed Bryson's arm. "What's happening?"

"I believe that other doctor must have given Don something in his IV to kill him."

Which meant Murdoc's tentacles had also reached into Alaska.

His spies were everywhere.

NINE

Jayla rubbed the throbbing goose egg on her forehead and drank from a water bottle as she sat in the station's lunchroom, trying to make sense of what had happened at the hospital. Somehow, Murdoc had discovered Don's whereabouts and had taken him out before he could tell them anything else about the criminal's operation. The Reese brothers were both dead at the hands of this man— or woman. Jayla and Bryson still weren't any closer to identifying Murdoc.

Bryson set a hot chocolate in front of her and sat. "You okay?"

"I could use some ibuprofen. You have any?"

"I do." Chris walked into the room and fished a bottle from his pocket. He dropped two in her hand. "There you go, beautiful." He sat, pulling the chair closer.

Really? We've just met.

She caught Bryson's squinched expression. Why the look?

Jayla ignored Chris's flirtation and popped the pills into her mouth, then took a drink from her water bottle. She wiggled her chair over slightly, irritation for this man taking up residence in her mind. Was it his actions, or was she being protective of Bryson? She buried the desire to harrumph at the crazy idea. Something she never thought she'd do. Stand up for the man who had put her friend in a wheelchair.

Concentrate, Jay. "Tell me, Chris—how long have you been a medic?"

"Ten years."

Bryson steepled his fingers. "What did you give Don? Apparently, the doctor said it may have caused his seizure."

Chris banged on the table. "It did not."

"What was it?" Bryson leaned closer, getting into Chris's face.

"A pain medication with codeine. That's it." He waggled his finger at Bryson. "What are you accusing me of, Clarke?"

"Why the loud voices?" Supervisor Thamesford marched into the room. "What's going on?"

Chris backed away from Bryson. "Clarke is accusing me of poisoning the prisoner."

"He did no such thing." There she went again, coming to his rescue, but she couldn't help it. "He only asked what meds you gave Don."

Chris bolted out of his chair. "Sure sounded like an accusation to me. I need to get to work." He stormed from the room.

"Clarke, you need to play nice in the sandbox." Leon joined them at the table.

Bryson raised his hands. "I did nothing wrong. Chris has been acting strange lately."

"And you haven't? Please don't tell me you're back on this avalanche conspiracy." Leon shifted his gaze to Jayla. "Does he have you believing it now, too?"

"It's not a conspiracy, sir. Don confirmed it when we questioned him." Jayla sipped her hot chocolate, gathering her thoughts on just how much information she should divulge. After all, everything pointed to a team of Murdoc's men on both sides of the border. She no longer trusted anyone after the attack on Jeff's chopper.

"What else did he say?" Leon asked.

"Only that he heard the words *avalanche* and *dynamite* when he was on the ridge," Bryson said.

She noted he'd left out the part about copper.

Seemed he also didn't trust his own team.

"Sir, where's Jeff?" Jayla asked. "We need to get back to our station and file a report."

"Still with the team, inspecting the crash."

Jayla's cell phone buzzed, and she checked the screen. Sergeant Park. She stood and raised her phone. "I need to take this." She hit Accept and walked out of the room. "Hi, Sergeant. I'm so sorry about Isaac."

"Thank you. Are you okay?" The man's broken voice revealed his deep sorrow.

"I'll be fine. Not sure yet when I'll be able to get back. The storm has intensified." She pinched the bridge of her nose.

"You need to be aware of another incident and get back here soon."

Jayla dropped her hand and stiffened. "What?"

"Fire at Philip's location."

Jayla's legs buckled, and she leaned against the wall to keep from falling. Someone had tried to take out her entire team, including the dogs. "Are they okay?" She held her breath, waiting to hear about Philip's condition, along with Stella's and Moose's.

"They're fine. They got out without injury, and I've relocated them farther off the grid. Fire chief said an accelerant was used to start the fire." He exhaled. "Jayla, what's going on? First the bomb at our kennel and now this. Why is someone targeting our dogs?"

"Not sure, sir. But I'm guessing they believe the dogs are a threat."

"Threat to what, though?"

She hesitated. How much should she share? "Not sure." An idea formed. "Sir, can you contact Faircord Junction's station and request that Supervisor Thamesford allow Bryson Clarke and I to work together?"

Now she'd officially asked for Bryson's help? Wow... He'd chipped away at her defenses in just over twenty-four hours.

"Why Clarke?"

"I can't share more without solid evidence, but he has a theory." Would he press her for more?

"Fine, I'll call him now. Just get back here as quick as you can—and, Jayla?"

She let out a breath. "Yes, sir?"

"You're in charge. For now. Please keep Hercules safe and off the radar."

"Will do." She ended the call and walked back into the room, where Bryson and Leon were in a heated debate.

Leon's cell phone rang, and he fished it from his pocket, studying the screen. "Your leader. I'm guessing this is your doing, Jayla?" He answered the call as he left the room.

Bryson smirked. "What did you do?"

"Requested your help back in the Yukon." She leaned down and kissed Herc's forehead. "We've had another attack on our dogs, but they're okay." She gave Herc another kiss and stood. "Bryson, someone is targeting our dogs. Any ideas as to why?"

"They're SAR and have rescued avalanche victims. Do you think it's Murdoc?" He rubbed his chin. "It makes little sense."

"And it may not even be Murdoc."

"True, but my gut is telling me it's related to whatever business he's in." His eyes widened. "Wait. Don mentioned copper. Do you think they're mining for copper in our mountains?"

"In the winter? Why would they hide it?"

"Copper is highly sought after, so I'm guessing Murdoc stumbled upon it and wants it all to him—or her—self."

Jayla walked back to the table and finished drinking her hot chocolate. "Do we know if copper is in our mountains?"

Leon stormed back into the room and pointed to Bryson. "Seems Sergeant Park has requested your presence in the Yukon." He turned to Jayla. "Your boss is very persuasive."

"Yup, that's him. Ethan used to say the man always got his way and there was no use in arguing." Tears over her lost friend welled up, but she kept them at bay. There would be time to mourn later. Right now, they had a job to do.

"Clarke, you're good to leave and work with Jayla." The supervisor took a step toward the door and turned. "But keep me updated—and if you need help, reach out."

"Yes, sir."

The man left.

"Well, looks like I'm coming with you. We can take my four-wheel drive, as we'll need it in this storm and it's fully equipped. I keep it stocked in case of emergencies. You never know what can happen in the wintertime." He grimaced.

"What is it?"

"I need to plan for Avery to stay with my parents again. My dad is going to give me an earful." He pulled out his phone. "Wait. I need to stop at their place. We can also talk to my mom about copper. She's a geologist."

"Perfect. I'll see where Jeff is."

"I'm here." Jeff walked into the room, holding a bagged object. "You'll never guess what we found in the wreckage."

"That appears to be a tracking device." Bryson held out his hand. "Let me see."

Jeff gave it to him. "That's exactly what it is. Someone wanted to know precisely where we were in order to launch that RPG." He paused. "We also found the spot where the suspect fired it from. Local authorities are examining it closer, but I'm sure they won't find anything."

Heat coursed through Jayla's neck, knotting her muscles.

How could they stay off Murdoc's radar long enough for them to figure out his identity and protect Ogilwyn Mountain Pass?

Bryson parked beside his father's cruiser and cringed. He had hoped he wouldn't have to deal with Lieutenant Trent Clarke, but it seemed the man was home on a break. Thankfully, his mom worked out of their house, as they wanted to get her opinion on copper mines in the area. He shut off the engine and turned to Jayla. "I'll warn you—my father can be rough."

"He can't be worse than my dad." She unbuckled her seat belt.

"Well, you can see for yourself." He exited his car, and they approached the house.

Too Tall had told Jayla he wanted to stay for a bit and work with the crew still scouring the site. He'd find a way back to Canada on his own.

Thamesford had taken the tracking device to their local authorities to dust for prints.

"How far do you and Avery live from here?" Jayla asked.

"Not far enough." He chuckled. "Around the corner. It's handy with Avery, though."

An icy gust of wind snaked down Bryson's back, reminding him of the weather. A break in the system would allow them to get back into Canada before it turned dangerous again. Plows had been out for the past few hours, struggling to keep the roads clear. Hopefully they'd succeeded.

"Let's go inside, as we need to make this quick." He pointed to the clouds. "Storm isn't over yet."

Jayla opened the back. "Hercules, come."

The dog jumped out and followed Jayla to the front door. Bryson held it open for the pair. "After you."

A welcome wave of heat wafted out, bringing with it the scent of a roaring fire. The Clarke household used wood logs. His father had always insisted on it; and Bryson, too, preferred the real McCoy. It reminded him of fun times during summer campouts and s'mores.

He stepped inside and closed the door. "Mom? You here?"

His father appeared around the corner, hands on hips. "What, you don't want to talk to me?"

I don't have time to argue. That's why I want to see Mom. "We need her expertise." Bryson turned to Jayla. "This is my dad, Lieutenant Trent Clarke. Dad, this is Jayla Hoyt and Hercules."

The lieutenant stuck out his hand. "Nice to meet you. Heard lots about you."

Jayla shook his hand. "Hopefully it wasn't all bad." She turned back to Bryson, lifting a brow.

Bryson raised his hands. "Of course not."

"We heard about the chopper crash. Sorry about your coworker." He gestured them farther inside. "Come— your mother should be out in a minute. I'm just having a quick early supper before heading back to our station." He walked into the dining room.

Bryson's mother turned the corner. "So good to see you, dear." She stopped when she noticed Jayla. "Who's this?"

Jayla stuck out her hand. "Jayla Hoyt. I work on the

CBM task force. Nice to meet you." She pointed to her dog. "This is Hercules, my SAR partner."

"Dr. Shannon Clarke." His mother's eyes brightened, and she shook Jayla's hand before squatting in front of Hercules. "He's so handsome. Hey, bud. Nice to meet you."

Hercules stuck out his paw.

His mom giggled. "Oh, and he's clever."

"He's showing off," Jayla said.

"Mom, we need to ask you some questions." Bryson nudged Jayla into the dining room. "Do you have a minute?"

"For you? Of course." She followed him into the room. "What's going on?"

Bryson caught them up-to-date on what was happening on their mountain pass. "Are you aware of any copper ore mines in the area?"

"Not in Alaska. Some near Whitehorse, though." She poured herself a cup of coffee from the carafe. "Why?"

"We think someone has found deposits in the mountains and is secretly mining copper."

His father whistled. "There certainly would be money in the black market for it."

"Mom, can you put some feelers out? I know you're well-connected across both Alaska and the Yukon." He snatched a cookie from a plate. "Have one, Jayla. Mom makes the best chocolate chip cookies." He took a bite.

She nibbled on one. "He's not lying. These are divine."

"Glad you like them." She patted Bryson's hand. "Yes, I'll definitely ask around and get back to you. They wouldn't be mining in the winter, though. Perhaps marking spots to mine during the summer months?"

"Maybe." He stole a look at his father. *Now for the big question.* He inhaled deeply. "Mom, Dad... We need your help with something else, too."

He tried to soften the blow by using *we*.

"What is it, son?" An edge sounded in his father's tone. The pleasant "company is here" voice had disappeared.

"Our leaders have agreed for Jayla and I to work together on this case. I need to head back to the Yukon with her. I'm not sure how long I'll be gone."

His father's eyes darkened. "Not again. You know how—"

His mother rested her hand on her husband's. "Trent, Avery will be fine. Bryson's work is important. Give him a break."

Thank you, Mom.

The front door opened and closed.

Avery was back from school.

His dad stood. "Fine. But *you* break it to your niece. I have to go back to work." He left.

Voices sounded before Avery appeared in the entryway.

Bryson got up and hugged his niece. "Squirt, I'm so glad you're here. I want you to meet my friends." He released her and nudged the shy girl toward the dining room table.

"This is Jayla and Hercules."

Jayla crouched in front of his niece. "So nice to meet you, Avery. You have beautiful hair."

Avery fingered her blond locks. "Thank you. You too."

Ruff!

"Hercules would like to say hello. Is that okay?"

Avery stumbled back.

"He won't hurt you, sweetie." She turned to Hercules. "Stay."

He sat.

"Let him smell your hand, Squirt." Bryson squatted.

Avery gingerly held out her hand.

Hercules sniffed before licking her.

Avery giggled and snatched her hand back. "He's funny. Why does he have a vest on?"

"He's my partner," Jayla said. "He helps me find people who are lost."

"Cool."

Jayla removed the dog's rescue vest. "Would you like to pet him?"

Avery nodded.

Jayla took his niece's hand and rubbed it on top of Hercules's head.

Avery's eyes widened. "He's soft."

Bryson's heart hitched. Jayla's gentleness with Avery played on his emotions. If only—

Stop.

He stood. "Squirt, can I talk to you?" Time to divert his attention to the task at hand, not silly thoughts of Jayla. "How was school today?"

"Boring." She unzipped her book bag. "I got all my math questions right!" She held out a sheet of homework.

"That's awesome. I'm so proud of you." Bryson kissed her forehead. "Listen, Uncle Bry has to go back to Canada."

"Aw… Can't Jayla and Hercules stay here tonight?"

What? Where did that come from?

His gaze switched to Jayla's.

Her full lips turned upward into a radiant smile, her beauty capturing his attention.

Wait—had he just thought about her lips and dreamed of kissing them?

He cleared his throat and addressed Avery. "We have to work in Canada right now, Squirt." He motioned toward his mother. "You'll be staying at Gramma's. Is that okay?"

"Can I watch another movie?"

"Of course you can, sweetie," his mom said. "I'll make you cheddar popcorn this time. Sound good?"

The blonde jumped up and down. "Yay!"

"Thanks, Mom. You still have lots of clothes for her here?"

"I do."

"Good." Bryson once again squatted in front of the seven-year-old he now thought of as a daughter and hugged her. "I'm not sure how long I'll be gone, but remember how much I love you."

She squeezed tighter. "To the moon and back."

"Exactly." He released her. "You be good for Grams and Gramps, okay?"

She rolled her eyes. "Uncle Bry, you know I will."

Jayla snickered.

"Time to go. I need to stop at my place first and grab some things." He walked over to his mom and kissed her cheek. "Thanks."

"Anytime. You know that." She wrapped her arm around him. "I like Jayla. She's pretty," she whispered.

That she is, Mom. That she is.

He backed away and threw a mock scowl at his mom. She shrugged.

Avery hugged the retriever. "Bye, Hercules." Next, she threw her arms around Jayla's legs. "Bye, Jayla. Will you come back and play with me soon?" Her big blue eyes fluttered, pleading with Jayla.

She knows how to win hearts.

Ouch. The thought of that as she grew older stabbed at his heart.

"You betcha, sweetie." Jayla extended her hand toward his mother. "Dr. Clarke, thank you for looking into the matter for us."

"Of course. Call me Shannon, dear." She patted Jayla's hand before releasing it. "I agree with my granddaughter—come back anytime."

Wow. A double invitation.

Jayla didn't stand a chance with these two.

Twenty minutes later, after packing a duffel bag, Bryson turned onto the Alcan Highway, which connected Alaska and the Yukon.

"Your family seems nice," Jayla said. "Avery is a sweetie."

"She is, and I can't believe how fast she bonded with you. Normally, she's shy with strangers."

"What can I say? It's my magnetic personality." Jayla laughed at her joke.

He studied her profile. "You'd make a great mother."

Her mouth dropped open.

Did he really just say that out loud? *What's wrong with you, Bry?*

"Sorry, I didn't mean to—"

Crunch!

Bryson's grip tightened on the wheel as he stole a glance in the rearview mirror.

A dark blue SUV with tinted windows was preparing to ram them a second time.

"Hang on!" Bryson accelerated.

The SUV matched his speed and smashed into his bumper again.

His vehicle skidded into the path of an oncoming transport truck.

Bryson's state trooper driver's training kicked in, and he swerved, praying the tire traction would hold on the icy road.

And keep them out of the path of a deadly collision with an 18-wheeler.

TEN

Jayla held her breath as the truck's horn blared. She clung to the grab handle and prayed for their safety. *Lord, please hear me. Save us.* How many times had she cried out to God in the past twenty-four hours?

Herc's bark from the back seat reminded her they weren't in a K-9 vehicle.

"Hercules, cover!" She had taught him to lie low with the sound of the word *cover.*

Bryson swerved the vehicle, but the tires yanked them back toward the truck like moths to a sprouting flame. He hit the wheel. "Come on!"

The driver once again blew the horn and veered in the ditch's direction. Its tires caught and the semi's left wheels lifted. If the driver didn't get control and turn the truck back onto the road, it would tip.

Jayla held her breath.

He compensated and the truck righted itself, continuing down the road.

Bryson finally got his vehicle under control as the blue SUV shot around them and sped down the highway. He pressed his radio button and called in a description of the suspect's vehicle. "That was too close for comfort."

Jayla let out an audible breath and nodded.

Bryson's cell phone rang through the Bluetooth, and "Faircord Junction Dispatch" appeared on the screen. He hit Accept. "Clarke here."

"We have a situation," Dispatch said.

Jayla froze. She wasn't sure she could take anything else today.

"What's happening?" Bryson asked.

"Avalanche on Elimac Mountain. Two skiers were reported missing."

Bryson looked at her. "That's on the border, north of our location."

"Supervisor Thamesford wanted me to call, as we need Hercules. Our dogs are all out on other calls and too far away."

"Understood." Jayla shifted in her seat. "How long ago did the avalanche happen?"

"Three minutes. Friends of the skiers were with them and called us immediately. They were on a different ski hill when it happened but saw the avalanche carry their friends down. You need to get there quickly. They're running out of time. Clarke, we've also dispatched a team to meet you there."

"Thanks. We're on our way." Bryson punched off the call and took an exit to change their course. "I hope the suspect who ran us off the road is long gone. We can't have them interfering."

"What equipment do you have in the back?"

"Everything. My skis, beacons, airbag, shovels, flare gun. Never leave without protection."

Five minutes later, they drove into the Elimac Mountain ski-chalet-and-lift area. A young man stopped shoveling the entranceway and observed their approach.

Jayla opened the back door. "Hercules, come. Time to work, bud."

The dog hopped out, wagging his tail.

Bryson retrieved his skis and handed her a backpack. "You can rent skis here, thankfully."

"Do you know this mountain well?" Jayla secured the bag on her back.

"Some. I just have to find out exactly which hill the avalanche hit." He picked up his skis and approached the worker.

Jayla followed.

"How can I help you?" The younger man spied Hercules. "Oh, you're the group here to find the skiers."

"Yes." Bryson stuck out his gloved fist. "I'm Ranger Bryson Clarke. This is Jayla Hoyt and Hercules from Canada."

The young man fist-bumped Bryson. "I'm Howie. Nice to meet you."

"Which run were the skiers on when the avalanche happened?" Bryson asked. "We were on our way to Canada when the call came in, so we don't have many details. The rest of my team should arrive soon."

"They're already here. Said they were in the area patrolling when Dispatch called them. They took the lift to Gil Run a few minutes ago."

Bryson held up his radio. "What channel are you on, in case we need to get in touch with you while we're on the mountain?"

"The reception can be spotty at times, so beware." He gave him the information before setting his shovel aside. He addressed Jayla. "I'll get you skis. Size?"

"Seven."

Howie hurried around the corner.

"Chris and Faith sure made it here fast, even if they were in the area." Bryson put his boots on. "Man, I shouldn't be so suspicious of my team." He snapped the buckles shut.

"It's understandable. We don't know who we can trust." She bent down and stroked Herc. "This guy is the only one I trust."

Bryson popped upward. "Wait... You don't trust me yet—even after everything we've been through?"

His tone conveyed his hurt feelings, but the tortured look on his handsome face wrestled with her heart.

Oops. *Jay, you messed up again.*

She stood. "I'm learning to, but I keep remembering how you froze when the grizzly attacked Julie. That's hard to come back from, Bryson."

"Don't you think it still bothers me every day? I keep running *what-if* scenarios through my head—but my counselor told me in order to move forward, I need to deal with the past. I'm trying to do that." He picked up his skis. "I'll be at the gondola's base."

He walked away, leaving her in staled silence.

Good job, Jayla. Why couldn't she put it behind her?

Truth be told, she had a hard time forgiving herself for not only Julie's accident but also Michael's and Kyle's suicides. She also kept *what-if* scenarios running through her mind. If only she'd been a better sister and fiancée. If only she'd come through the clearing when the grizzly attacked first. If only she hadn't taken that isolated road while on a special mission. Too many *what-if*s. Was there anything she could have done to prevent these situations from happening? She worked hard at redeeming herself for those mistakes but had failed miserably.

Redemption is not your job.

She sucked in a breath. Where did that thought come from?

Howie approached with skis and boots. "Here you go."

"Appreciate it." Thankful for the interruption from her thoughts, she stepped into the boots. No more time for self-pity. "Hercules, come."

Jayla found Bryson leaning against the lift building. "Listen, I'm sorry. I didn't mean to bring the past up again."

"I understand, though. Really, I do. I just had hoped we were moving past it." He pushed off the wall. "We need to go." He walked toward the gondola car.

She and Herc followed him and climbed into the sheltered ski lift.

How could she tell him her ice wall was thawing when it came to him, especially after seeing him around Avery? His gentleness toward the little girl had ignited a longing within her she thought had died along with Michael. So why did she drive him away? Deep down, she knew the answer.

She feared getting hurt. Feared having her heart ripped apart. It was something she never wanted to go through again. Perhaps she didn't deserve happiness.

The motion jolted her back to the moment. The lift slowly rose and soon kissed the snow-covered treetops. If it wasn't for their precarious situation, she would have enjoyed the breathtaking view.

Right now, she must apologize and ease the thick tension blocking the man beside her. "I'm sorry, Bryson. I am moving forward since yesterday. Little bits at a time. Can you forgive my stupid remark?"

He smiled. "I'm not mad. I just—"

A shot pierced through the ski lift's glass, silencing him.

He threw his arm on top of her and shoved her forward. "Stay down!"

Her heartbeat ricocheted as her stomach twisted into an impregnable knot. She gripped Hercules and held him tight as thoughts zipped through her mind.

They were trapped with nowhere to run...

Or hide.

Bryson stayed low, sheltering Jayla. He extracted his radio and hit the talk button. "Elimac Station, this is

Ranger Clarke, heading up your ski lift. We're taking on shots. Can you get us to the top faster?"

Another gunshot penetrated the gondola's window.

How many more bullets before it shattered?

"Howie here. Increasing speed."

The car lurched and sped up.

Bryson peeked out the window and caught movement below in the trees north of the ski chalet. "Call 911. Shooter is north of your building. Hurry."

"Copy that," Howie said.

Finally, silence permeated the car, and Jayla shifted beneath him. "Is he still out there? Can I get up? I need to check Herc."

He removed his arm. "I think we're out of range now, but stay low just in case."

She crawled over to Hercules and guided her hands over his body. "I don't feel any injuries. You good, Hercules?"

He barked.

Jayla kissed his forehead. "Good boy."

Bryson loved their powerful bond. Herc was like a child to her, and her gentleness with the dog impressed him.

The gondola clanged to a halt at the top, and the doors slid open.

Bryson crouched and unholstered his weapon, pointing it in all directions as he scanned the terrain. He punched his radio button. "Howie, close your ski lift. I don't want anyone else on the mountain right now."

"The boss won't like it, but I understand, Ranger Clarke. Safety first."

Smart kid.

"Bry, we need to get to those skiers quickly," Jayla said. "They're running out of time."

Wait. Had Jayla called him by his nickname? No time to think about what that meant. He had a job to do.

Bryson holstered his weapon. "Coast is clear."

He stepped outside and spotted Ramsay and Faith standing beside a tree in a heated conversation.

What was going on?

Did this pair have something to do with the shooting? *Bryson, don't jump to conclusions. They're your fellow team members and trained to save lives, not take them.*

He put on his skis and approached the duo. "We were just shot at on the ride up here. You guys see anything?"

Ramsay shook his head. "No, but we thought we heard gunfire."

"Sniper?" Faith asked, settling her hand on her holster.

"Yes, but probably long gone now." Bryson did another perimeter sweep, but nothing out of the ordinary appeared in his line of vision.

Jayla skied toward them, holding Hercules's leash as he ran beside her. They stopped shy of their location. "Where was the avalanche, and did the other skiers report where their friends were when it happened?"

Faith pointed. "Down Gil Run. That way. And yes, they saw the snow bury them three-quarters of the way down the mountain."

"Okay, I'm taking Hercules to that point."

Bryson turned to Ramsay. "Let's go. We'll need your medical expertise."

The medic nodded. "Right behind ya."

Bryson followed Jayla and Herc down the mountain. The dog impressed Bryson as he stayed in a tight Olympic-style formation with his handler as he ran between her legs. Obviously, a method they'd practiced many times.

The group stopped when they reached the three-quarter mark.

Jayla unhooked the dog. "Hercules, search!"

Hercules bounded through the snow, crisscrossing as

he searched. Moments later, he stopped and dug quickly as his tail spun high in the air.

"He's found something!" Jayla yelled, skiing over to where Hercules was digging.

Bryson followed and dropped to his knees, paddle-shoveling.

Lord, help us find them alive.

Wait—did he just pray?

Jayla prayed as she dug deeper to reach the skier Herc had found. She had given him the command to search again to find the second victim. They were running out of time. Finally, they uncovered a foot. "Quick, we're almost there."

Bryson, Faith and Chris dug faster, and they soon pulled the male from the snow. Chris immediately began rescue breaths. Within seconds, the victim coughed. *Thank You, Lord.*

One found, one more to go.

Herc barked.

Jayla turned toward her dog's cry. Once again, he buried his head in the snow, digging with all his might as his tail twirled like a helicopter's blade.

"Herc's found the other victim." Jayla pointed. "Let's go."

Bryson and Jayla dug alongside Herc. Minutes later, they reached the female victim and hauled her out from the snow coffin.

Jayla brushed the snow from her face, clearing her airway. She checked her vitals. No pulse. No breath. Jayla gave the young woman five rescue breaths.

Nothing.

"Chris! Help. She's not responding." Jayla was com-

petent in first aid but realized he had more training and
would know best.

Chris staggered over, trudging through the deep snow,
and dropped to his knees. "Give me room."

Jayla walked away, bringing Herc and rewarding him
with his toy. "Good boy."

She observed Chris as he attempted to resuscitate the
woman. After a few minutes, he turned to them and shook
his head.

She was gone.

The male skier made his way over to the female and
dropped into the snow. "No! Bring her back to me. We just
got engaged this morning."

Jayla's hand flew to her mouth. *Lord, why? Why take
away this man's happiness?* She stifled any further questions, as God wasn't listening. She approached the man,
kneeled and embraced him. "I'm so sorry for your loss."
She'd keep her condolences at her simple statement. She
refused to give the man the pat answers others had given
her at Michael's funeral.

He sobbed as she rocked him in her arms.

Herc dropped his toy and snuggled close. Was it his
way of apologizing for not finding the fiancée sooner?
Bud, it's not your fault. Jayla caressed her dog in reassurance of a job well done.

"Sir, we need to take you to the hospital to get you
checked out further." Chris packed up his medical equipment.

"Give him a minute," Bryson said. "He just lost the
love of his life."

Faith stood with her hands on her hips. "We need to
get away from the avalanche site in case another one hits.
The weather is iffy."

The man pulled away from Jayla. "This avalanche didn't

happen because of the weather. An explosion triggered it."
He pointed to his fiancée, his expression crumbling. "She was murdered."

Bryson inched closer. "Why would you say that? Did you see something?"

He pointed north. "We found a cave over there and heard men talking. They spotted us and started shooting. We skied away from them, but not before I saw them light dynamite. That's what triggered the avalanche."

Jayla's gaze whipped over to Bryson's. His widened eyes told her he'd surmised the same thing.

Murdoc had struck again.

This time on the Alaska–Yukon border.

He was killing people to hide whatever operation he had going in their mountain pass.

Heat assaulted Jayla's neck even in the frigid temperatures as she squared her shoulders, rallying her valor.

I will stop you, Murdoc, if it's the last thing I do.
For this man and for Ethan.

ELEVEN

Bryson studied his coworkers' faces after the skier's claim of murder. Faith's open mouth gave away her shock, while Ramsay's flattened lips revealed another story. Was he angry because of the senseless man-made avalanche or because he was involved and wanted to keep whatever evil deed happening in their mountains a secret? Either way, Bryson wanted to see this cave without their prying eyes. He had to get them off the mountain.

Forty minutes later, after the coroner removed the body, Bryson approached his coworker. "Chris, can you and Faith take the skier back to the chalet and get him checked out?"

"What are you going to do?" Ramsay straightened his arms at his side.

His reaction told Bryson it wouldn't be easy to get around the man's suspicions. "Jayla and I will ensure the area is safe. Make sure no other victims were buried." He left out the part about exploring the cave. Would he buy it?

Ramsay shifted his eyes to stare at Jayla before turning back to Bryson, inching closer. "You have a crush on her, don't you?"

That's where he went? Well, Bryson could admit that he admired the mountain survivalist, but right now, finding those responsible for another avalanche was his number one priority. "I need her and Herc's expertise. Please make sure no one else comes up the mountain until we know more. Got it?"

"What are you hiding?" Ramsay poked him in the chest. "You still suspect someone sabotaged the mountain? The skier is wrong. His fiancée's death has him imagining what really happened."

Or you want us to think that.

"Perhaps." Bryson stepped back into his skis. "But remember, someone shot at us earlier. Something's fishy, and I just want to make sure."

"Don't come up with more conspiracy ideas. You know Thamesford wouldn't like you interfering in something that doesn't exist and putting our station at risk." He walked over to Faith and the male skier. "Let's head out."

What? Had his leader told Ramsay about Bryson looking into the avalanches? Mistrust once again prickled the back of Bryson's neck.

Jayla skied up to Bryson's location. "What was that about?"

"Not entirely sure. I don't trust Ramsay. Something's off with him." Bryson looped his pole straps around his wrists. "Let's go look for this supposed cave. Hard to say if we'll find anything, since the skier said they set off dynamite."

"I'll follow you." She turned to her dog. "Hercules, come."

After searching for thirty minutes, Bryson stopped near a group of spruce trees and waited for Jayla.

She skied up to him and lowered her goggles. "Ready to give up?"

"Is Hercules trained in detecting explosives?" he asked.

"No. Just search and rescue, plus some protective skills I trained him on." Jayla rubbed the K-9's back. "You were hoping he'd smell the dynamite?"

Bryson took off his helmet and scratched the top of his head. "Yes. I want to find that cave. I believe the skier. It has to be around here somewhere. What are we missing?"

"Listen, I know you're frustrated. Maybe we should call it a day. You know what they say about fresh eyes, right?"

"I do, but—"

Suddenly, Hercules growled.

Movement to their right stiffened every muscle in Bryson's body. Was the shooter back? Bryson extracted his weapon, motioning for Jayla to remain quiet.

Hercules growled again.

Something had caught the dog's attention.

Jayla gestured to the right. "Over there."

A lynx skulked behind a tree.

Hercules barked.

Bryson clenched his fists. The cat would probably not attack unless provoked, and right now, they had to keep the dog from chasing after the animal. He pointed to a group of trees beside a rock formation. "Keep Hercules close. Let's slowly move over there to get out of the lynx's sight."

Jayla nodded.

The group inched forward and then huddled around the tree–rock formation.

Seconds later, the animal crept by, only yards away from them. Would Hercules bark? Bryson held his breath and motioned for Jayla to stay low. He flattened himself.

"Hercules, quiet." Jayla's whispered command seemed too loud. She sprawled on her belly.

Remarkably, the dog obeyed.

Bryson fingered his weapon but readied himself in case action was required. He would not let an animal attack happen again on his watch, especially with the beautiful woman nearby.

He observed the cat's motions across from their location and spied a strange formation—a pile of different-size rocks. Could it be hiding the cave? He fought the urge to go check it out and stayed motionless in their hiding spot. He didn't want to spook the lynx.

Five minutes had passed with no further cat sightings. "I think we're in the clear." Bryson stood.

"That was close." Jayla stumbled to her feet and brushed off the snow.

"Yes, and something my mother would call a *God thing*."

"What do you mean?" Jayla tugged on Hercules's leash. The dog jumped up and shook off the snow.

"See that formation over there?" He pointed. "I never would have seen that if we hadn't hidden from the lynx at the angle we did. It might be the cave. Come on."

They skied over as Hercules ran beside them.

Bryson removed his skis and walked to the group of rocks and branches. He pushed the snow-covered shrubbery away, exposing a crack in the formation. "Help me get these rocks out of the way. I can see an opening."

After clearing the blocked hole, Bryson withdrew his flashlight from the backpack and shined it through. The cave dropped meters away from the entrance, but he spotted equipment inside. He turned back to Jayla. "This is what the skier referred to. You and Hercules stay here. I'm not sure how safe it is."

"Not on your life. I love animals, but I'm not staying out here alone with that lynx still lurking." She held Hercules's leash close to her body. "After you."

"Stay right behind me, okay?"

She saluted. "Yes, sir." She dropped her hand. "Kidding. Let's go."

Bryson ducked and entered the cave. Knowing they wouldn't get too far in ski boots, he grabbed the stone wall and carefully proceeded down into the cave. Dampness sent shivers into his already-chilled body. Although he was used to cold weather, the prolonged hours of it sank deep into his bones.

He ignored the crisp air and shined his light around. Stacks of dynamite and multiple piles of chipped rocks cluttered the area. He shifted the beam to the walls. "There are different colors in the rock formation." He inched closer and handed her the light. "Hold this. I want to take pictures to send to Mom later so she can give us her opinion on it."

Bryson took off his gloves and retrieved his cell phone, swiping the screen to bring it to life. He clicked on his camera. "Shine the light close."

"Wow. I see oranges, golds, greens intermixed. I'm certainly not an expert, but this has to be copper." Jayla held the light on a particular spot. "Look at this one."

He took multiple pictures. "Mom will confirm for sure."

After taking shots of the cave walls, they made their way back to the gondola and moved inside the car.

Bryson unclipped his radio. "Howie, Ranger Clarke here. We're ready. Bring us down."

"Roger that."

The car lurched, and they began their descent.

Bryson held on to the bar railing. "Pray for a more peaceful ride back down. Free of snipers."

Jayla's cell phone rang, and she took it out of her pocket. "Sergeant Park. I'm surprised I got a signal." She hit the speaker button. "Hi, Grant. You're on with Ranger Clarke, too, sir."

"Are you done with the avalanche investigation? I need you back here." His voice boomed in the small car.

"What's happened?" Jayla asked.

"Another avalanche." His voice quivered. "Jay—bur-ied—station."

Jayla recoiled against the seat and dropped her cell phone.

Her sergeant's broken words still revealed his message. Her station had been attacked.

Bryson wrapped an arm around her and held her tight. Was this an accident or…?

Murdoc wanted to cover up any evidence he thought they might have.

The gondola lift reached the bottom, jostling Jayla in Bryson's hold and bringing her back to reality. She straightened her shoulders and scooped up her phone. She must find out about her coworkers and K-9 unit. She checked her cell signal. Two bars. "Sir, did everyone get out?" She held her breath and waited for his response.

"Thankfully, yes. Most were out on patrol when it happened. The skeleton staff at the station saw it coming and evacuated."

Jayla exhaled. "What about skiers in the area?"

"Teams are out searching, but according to the reports coming in, most skiers were on runs on the other side of our station. I'm thankful, as this could have been a lot worse."

"Agreed." Her shoulders relaxed, relief settling. "Just wrapping up here."

"Jayla, be safe and don't trust anyone." *Click.*

What? Why would he say that? Did he know something they didn't? John Reese's words tumbled through her mind.

Murdoc has spies everywhere.

She curbed her emotions and pushed off the seat, determination commandeering her body. She attached Herc's leash and addressed Bryson. "We need to get back to Canada."

He picked up his skis and poles. "First, let's warm up by the fire in the chalet."

"Yes, I need to find Herc water and something to eat before the drive back."

Howie met them as they entered the chalet. "Everything okay on the mountain?"

Jayla stomped snow from her boots. "For now. Listen, do you have any veggies, stews or soups I can give my dog? Plus, water?" She removed her backpack. "I want something more than treats before we head out."

Howie's gaze bounced between her and Bryson. "You guys don't know?"

Jayla braced herself for more bad news. "What?"

"The road into the ski resort is blocked due to a smaller avalanche. It happened while you were on Gil Run, approximately ten minutes ago."

"Great. That's all we need—another delay." Jayla hung her coat on a peg mounted to the wall.

"Are crews working on getting it cleared?" Bryson asked.

"A team is on their way. Might be a couple of hours, though, before they unblock the road." Howie pointed to Herc. "And yes, I can find something for your dog. Plus, grab whatever you like for yourselves at the café—on the house." He headed toward a closed door.

"Jayla, I'll go get our footwear so we can get out of these ski boots. Grab me a tea and something to eat." Bryson dashed out the door.

Ten minutes later, the three sat beside the roaring fire, eating a well-deserved snack. Howie had found stew for Herc, and the retriever had scarfed it down before curling up by the hearth.

"This is so frustrating." Jayla sipped her hazelnut-flavored coffee and tensed. "Do you think someone intentionally set this one off, too, to keep us here?"

"Possibly. But why?"

Jayla eyed Herc. "We're at the center of this investigation, and somehow Murdoc knows it."

"Through his supposed spies, you mean?"

"Exactly." She bit into her apple fritter, letting the cinnamon flavor linger on her tongue.

"Well, nothing would surprise me now. Hopefully, the crew clears it soon." Bryson motioned toward Herc. "He sure is impressive. I loved the way he skied between your legs. That must have taken lots of practice."

"We do it to protect their paws from other skiers. It's now natural for us."

Bryson's phone rang as a video-chat call came through. He swiped his screen. "My mother's calling." He hit a button. "Hi, Mom."

"Hey, son. Is Jayla there, too? I want to talk to both of you about the pictures you sent. I've done some digging."

"She's here. Just a sec." Bryson sat next to Jayla and held the phone between them.

Jayla waved. "Hi, Dr. Clarke."

"Dear, remember—it's Shannon. You both okay? I heard about the avalanche. It's been on the news already."

"We're good, Mom. Did you identify the rock?"

"Definitely copper ore. A rare find here in Alaska, even if it was right on the Canadian border. My fellow geologists are checking, but so far there have been no reports of any federal mining claims logged."

Bryson huffed out a breath. "Of course not. They're doing it illegally. My guess is they're putting it on the black market to sell to the highest bidder."

"D—Shannon, do you know if any claims are logged in Canada along the Ogilwyn Mountain Pass?"

"I know a Canadian geologist in Whitehorse. I'll contact her and get back to you." A timer rang in the background.

"Gotta run. Supper's ready. Avery wanted lasagna tonight. Then we're watching a movie."

Bryson chuckled. "She has you wrapped around her pinkie, doesn't she?"

She winked. "Wouldn't have it any other way. You two stay safe."

"We will, Mom. Give Avery a kiss for me. Bye." He blew her a kiss.

His mother did the same before ending the video call.

Warmth spread into Jayla's body—both from the fireplace heat and the gentleness radiating on Bryson's face. Clearly, his relationship with his mother was strong, and when she'd mentioned Avery, his smile erupted.

And defrosted Jayla's heart. Who was she kidding? She was falling for the man beside her, even after her resolve to stay mad at him for his failure in Julie's grizzly attack.

"What?"

"Huh?" His question jolted her from thoughts of romance.

"You were staring." He smirked.

"Was not." She shifted in her chair. *Liar.* How could she not? Even after a horrific day, the man was still gorgeous. "Just tired."

He placed his hand on her arm. "I'll go see if Howie has an update on the road situation."

"Thanks." She stuffed the rest of her fritter in her mouth and sat back, closing her eyes. She required rest, too, after a long, tiring day. When would it end? She exhaled and sank deeper into the wingback chair.

"Jayla, wake up."

Bryson's voice sounded in the distance, but the gentle nudging on her arm revealed his close presence.

She jerked awake and strangled the armrest. She'd fallen asleep. "What time is it?"

"Eight fifteen. Ready to go? The road is clear. Howie and I are going to go check with the crew to ensure everything is okay. I'll meet you in the Jeep." He left the building.

Jayla pushed herself up and stretched. "Come on, Herc. Time to wake up."

He didn't respond.

She squatted and shook him. "Bud?"

Nothing.

Her heart rate catapulted and sent erratic jolts through her body. What was wrong with her dog? She ran her hands along his body and stopped as her fingers touched something obscure. She leaned closer. A tiny dart was lodged in Herc's leg.

"No! Come on, bud—"

"He can't hear you. Don't worry. He's okay—just a dose of a sleeping aid."

Jayla froze and slowly stood, turning toward the menacing voice.

However, she only spotted a flash of a masked man in an orange vest before a blunt object came down hard on her head—

Sending her into black nothingness.

TWELVE

Bryson approached his quiet vehicle. What was taking Jayla so long? He'd spoken to the crew for five minutes and had found out the road was now clear. Howie had officially closed the ski lifts but disappeared around the building. Bryson hurried back into the chalet.

And stilled in his tracks.

An unconscious Jayla lay beside the fireplace.

Hercules was nowhere in sight.

"Jayla!" Bryson rushed to her side and dropped to the floor, checking her vitals. Pulse and breathing strong. He nudged her shoulders. "Wake up!" He glanced around the room.

Something was wrong. No way would the dog leave Jayla's side.

He shook her again. "Come on, beautiful. Come back to me."

Had he just called her *beautiful*?

You have it bad, dude. Rein it in.

Finally, she stirred and opened her eyes. "What happened?"

"Not sure. When you didn't come to the Jeep, I came in to check on you. Where's Hercules?"

She flew upright, holding her head. "He drugged him."

"Who?" Bryson helped her into the chair. "Tell me what happened."

"I couldn't wake Herc, and someone approached from

behind, stating he'd drugged him. I found a dart buried on the inside of his leg." She rubbed her head. "Then something hit me hard."

"Wait. He didn't take you?" Bryson paused, reluctant to state the obvious. "He wanted Hercules."

"No!" Jayla stood quickly and teetered.

He wrapped his arm around her waist, catching her before helping her back into the chair. "You need to sit."

The chalet door opened.

Bryson pivoted and whipped out his gun.

Howie raised his hands. "Whoa. It's me. What's going on?"

"Someone attacked Jayla, and Herc is gone." Bryson took a step, keeping his weapon trained. "Was it you? Where have you been?"

"I was closing the ski lift building. I did not do this." He gulped. "I promise."

Jayla got up slowly. "Did you shoot my dog with a dart?"

"No! I—" He stopped.

"What is it?" Jayla asked.

Howie's eyes widened. "I remember seeing someone duck into the forest earlier when you were coming back into the lodge. I thought it was just someone exploring the wilderness."

Bryson examined the young man's face, but nothing in his expression made him suspicious. He holstered his weapon.

Jayla latched onto his arm. "Someone is following us and knew we wouldn't be able to leave, so the drug didn't react instantly. Could it be the sniper? Why would he take Herc?" Her voice wobbled, and she crumpled into the chair, sobbing.

Lord, I realize I'm the last person You should listen to, but can You find Hercules? Jayla needs him. Please.

Would God hear his prayer?

Bryson hurried back to her side and pulled her into an embrace. "We'll find him. I promise."

She pushed back. "How can you promise that? Why do bad things always happen to me when I'm around you?" She shoved him aside, jumped up from the chair and then yanked her coat from the rack before racing out into the night.

Bryson let out an audible exhale. She was right—he was a magnet for tragedy. First Ellie, then Jayla's friend.

No, God definitely wouldn't listen to him. Bryson was a failure.

Always a failure.

"Man, I'm sure she didn't mean it," Howie said. "This isn't your fault."

It wasn't? It wouldn't have happened if he'd kept them by his side.

"How can I help?"

Howie's question jerked Bryson into action, determination squaring his shoulders. "I'll call it in. Get all the flashlights you can. We need to check the perimeter. Maybe Hercules is still close."

Howie nodded and scurried from the room.

Bryson walked out of the chalet, phoning his father.

"What's going on, Bryson? Your mom told me about what you found."

"Dad, I need your help. Someone has taken Hercules. Can you arrange for a search party?" Bryson peered into the night sky. Snow once again pummeled the region.

Really? They just couldn't get any type of break.

"Son, the weather report isn't good. Another storm is moving in."

"Please try. Get the police here. Now!" He hung up and withdrew his flashlight. "Jayla, where are you?"

The wind spiraled around the building and coiled down Bryson's spine. He wanted to be back beside the fireplace, but right now, he had more pressing matters.

Find both Jayla and Hercules. Proving his worth would hopefully diminish her disdain for him.

He raised his flashlight and sprinted to the back of the building. "Jayla, where are you?"

His beam caught a form huddled beside the ski lift entrance. Bryson rested his hand on his gun and edged forward.

Jayla.

He ran over to her, falling to his knees in front of her. "I'm sorry. I shouldn't have left your side."

She lifted her head, revealing her tearstained face. "No, this isn't your fault, and I'm sorry for saying so. I didn't mean to take my worry over Herc out on you." She pushed herself to a standing position. "Bry, we need to find him. I can't lose him, too."

Who else had she lost? Was she referring to her younger brother, Kyle?

The sound of rushing footsteps came from behind them.

Bryson turned, his hand once again resting on his gun.

"It's me." Howie raised a flashlight in one hand and a lantern in the other. "This will help."

"Jayla, I've called my dad and asked he send a search party, but—"

"A storm is moving in. I can feel it in my chilled bones." She held her hand out to Howie. "Can I have the lantern?"

He gave it to her. "I'll help in any way I can."

"Thank you," Bryson said. "I'm sorry for accusing you earlier."

"I understand." He flicked the flashlight on. "Where do you want me to look?"

"Search and rescue is part of what we do on the Cross-

Border Mountain Task Force." Jayla raised the lantern. "But, Bryson, you and I both know they won't search tonight. Not with the storm moving back into the region. It's too dangerous in these conditions."

"Wait!" Howie swung his light toward the front. "I just remembered something else. I noticed fresh tire tracks earlier. At first, I thought you'd left, and then I noticed your Jeep. If it wasn't you, who was it? The road crew hadn't come this far in, and the ski lift has been closed for hours."

"Show me where." Bryson headed toward the driveway. The others followed.

Howie pointed. "There. Snow has covered it some, though."

Bryson bent down and examined the tracks. "These are from some sort of heavy truck." He sprang up. "Wait. The suspect must have posed as a road-crew worker. That's probably how they got by everyone."

"That's it. I remember seeing an orange vest before I passed out." Jayla expelled a breath, its vapors lingering in the cold air. "At least we know Hercules isn't out in the cold. For now, anyway."

Bryson removed his key fob from his pocket. "I want to follow these tracks before the police arrive and drive over them. Howie, can you remain here and let the police know what happened?" He pointed to his radio. "I'm still on the same channel."

"Got it. You guys go. Find Herc."

Bryson studied the direction of the tracks. "It appears they drove into the trees. Is there a road there? I don't remember seeing one."

Howie raised his light, revealing an opening in the forest. "A service road goes through the woods and back out onto the main road. It's not used much in the wintertime—only by snowmobiles."

"That's how they got by any remaining service workers. Come on, Jay." Bryson hit the key fob button and climbed inside his Jeep.

Jayla slammed her seat belt buckle into place. "Do you think they'd harm Herc?"

"I don't think they would have drugged him if they really wanted to hurt him." Bryson started the engine and backed out of his parking spot, then veered toward the trees.

"I hope you're right."

He reached over and gave her shoulder a quick squeeze. "We'll find him."

Bryson gripped the steering wheel tightly and drove into the narrow passage with one thought in mind.

He wouldn't stop until he brought Hercules back to Jayla, even if it meant risking his own life for the dog.

He'd do it.

For her.

Jayla leaned closer and peeked out the Jeep's windshield into the dark, stormy night. The snow had intensified since they'd discovered Herc was missing. It confirmed her thinking—the team wouldn't send out a party because of both the inclement weather and the late hour. Right now, Jayla and Bryson were Herc's only hope.

More tears welled up as all the losses in her life slammed through her, threatening to spill out like a waterfall over a dam. First Kyle, then Michael and Ethan. Add Julie's and Dekker's injuries to the list and she had a colossal stack of bad memories careening through her mind. They would soon overpower her if she didn't restrain herself—and fast.

But how could she help it? Her beloved dog was out there somewhere. Alone with a madman. She prayed for Herc to regain his strength. Maybe he'd be able to escape.

Hope surged through her just as she noticed the tracks on the road disappear. "Stop." She pointed. "They end here."

Bryson put the Jeep in Park and removed his flashlight from the console. "Let's get a closer look."

They exited and walked to the front of the vehicle. Jayla shined her light, hoping to see more tracks, but either the snow had filled them in or—

Someone had approached through the forest.

"Bryson, do you think someone met them here and took Herc?"

He waved his light over the region, studying the areas around and under his vehicle. He walked farther down to the curve in the road before turning back. "It appears they backed up and swerved into the trees and out this way." He pointed. "The tracks continue toward the main road."

"What are we missing?" Jayla moved her light's beam in different directions.

Another set of tracks under a large branch were caught in her beam. "Wait... Look at this." She approached the imprint and bent low. "Snowmobile tracks. The branch sheltered it from the falling snow."

Bryson trudged over to her location. "The truck met an accomplice and took Hercules on a snowmobile—but where did they go?" He stood and swept his light around. "Wait, the tracks are heading in that direction. They're faint, as the snow covered them quickly. Let's go back to the chalet and talk to Howie again. See what other roads or buildings are in this area. I'm not familiar with these northern parts."

"But I need to keep going."

He helped her stand. "Jay, we don't know where they went. You know searching blindly never ends well. We need a plan."

Her head told her he was right, but her heart disagreed.

Her shoulders slumped in defeat as she got into his Jeep. Her weary limbs melted into the seat as nausea rose, threatening to overpower her emotions. She gazed out the window at the increasing snowfall. Her heart sank. There definitely wouldn't be any more searching tonight—not in this weather.

Minutes later, they parked beside a police cruiser and scrambled out.

Howie and a stout officer leaned against the car, chatting. Another officer inspected the area.

The trooper pushed off his vehicle and approached Bryson. "You Ranger Clarke?"

"I'll go make us some hot drinks." Howie entered the chalet.

"Yes, and this is Canadian mountain-survival specialist Jayla Hoyt," Bryson said.

"You are?" She held out her hand, but the officer barely acknowledged her presence.

Why?

"Name's Trooper Sanders. Your dad called our sergeant. Made us come out in this blasted storm. There's no sign of a sniper in the area." He gestured toward the opening in the woods. "You find anything?"

"Not a lot. More questions than answers." Bryson pointed to the entrance. "How about we go inside where it's warm and the snow isn't pelting our faces?"

"Good plan." Sanders turned to the younger officer. "Nathaniel. Inside."

Jayla shuffled through the doorway, making her way to the comfy chair beside the fireplace. She plunked herself down and removed her gloves before holding her hands close to the coals.

Bryson followed and sat next to her. "You okay?"

"Exhausted and frustrated." She turned to him. "You're

right—a search party will need to wait until daylight. But that's way too many hours that Herc will be out there alone."

"Do you want to pray?"

She tilted her head. "*You* want to pray?"

He shrugged.

She shifted her gaze back to the roaring fire. "Not sure it would help, anyway. God and I haven't been on great terms since—" How much more did she want to share?

"Since when?"

She slouched back in the chair. "Never mind."

The officers appeared with coffees in their hands. They each sat on separate sofas.

Howie followed, carrying a steaming hot chocolate. "For you, Jayla—with a cherry on top."

"Thanks." She took a sip.

"Tea for you, Bryson." Howie passed it to him before sitting in a rocking chair.

If Jayla wasn't so tired and worried about Herc, she'd enjoy the chalet's setting. The living room area set up around the fireplace created a skier's dream ambience after a day of being out in the cold. The café to the left featured fresh coffees, teas, hot chocolate, and bistro-style sandwiches and pastries. A place to unwind and chat with fellow outdoorsmen.

"Tell us what you found or didn't find." Trooper Sanders drank from his coffee mug. "This is Nathaniel. I'm teaching him the ropes."

Bryson reached over and shook the young redhead's hand. "Nice to meet you. We found a spot in the road where the truck stopped, and there are indications that a snowmobile was hidden under a large group of branches."

"We feel someone met the suspect and handed Herc off to whoever waited under the trees." The premeditated plan niggled at Jayla. How did they know they would still be here this time of day?

"Howie, are there any other roads or paths in those woods?" Bryson asked.

"Lots. But not too many people venture in that direction."

"Why not?" Jayla plucked the cherry from the whipped cream and popped it into her mouth.

"The terrain is rough. Lots of trees, some lakes, cliffs. You name it, this area has it. Including our own resident wilderness man."

Bryson hunched forward. "Your *what*?"

"Bertie, Gil Run's recluse, who lives in a cabin up on the ridge along with his hound dog, Mya. Such a kind man. He owns some of the private land up there."

Jayla jumped out of her chair. "Can we call him now? See if he's seen Herc?"

"He doesn't have a phone. Only a radio." Howie checked his watch. "Besides, it's well past nine, so he'd be in slumberland and have it turned off."

"Plus, you don't know which way these perps took your pet. You're barking up the wrong tree. Why are you so worried about a dumb dog?" Trooper Sanders walked over to the café and pulled out a cookie from the enclosed case. He stuffed his treat into his mouth before sitting back down.

Jayla fixed her gaze on Bryson.

His raised brow at the officer's blatant dismissal of both her and her idea had surprised him, too.

Did this older officer not like women, or was it the fact that she was from Canada and knew law enforcement? Her search and rescue skills placed her well within those boundaries.

She resisted the urge to give him a piece of her mind. The sudden throbbing in her head reminded her of her earlier run-in with the assailant. She rubbed the base of her skull. "Howie, do you have any pain medication?"

He hopped up. "On it."

Bryson leaned forward. "You okay?"

"I will be once we find Herc."

"Trooper Sanders, Jayla Hoyt is the best in the business, and I'll have you know this 'dumb dog,' as you call him, has saved many lives on our mountain pass." Bryson crossed his arms, sitting back. "You better mind your manners, or I'll have my father call your sergeant again. This time, the wrath of Lieutenant Trent Clarke will rain down upon you so hard you won't know what hit you."

Jayla placed her hand over her mouth, hiding the smirk she'd failed to stop. She liked this side of Alaska State park ranger Bryson Clarke. Perhaps he *had* changed.

Nathaniel smiled.

Seemed he also enjoyed seeing Bryson putting his fellow unprofessional officer in his place.

Trooper Sanders lurched upright. "Well, I can see you have everything under control here, Ranger Clarke. A search and rescue team will arrive early in the morning." He turned to his partner. "We're leaving." He stormed out of the chalet without waiting for a response.

The rookie officer shrugged. "Sorry. He's a dweeb and had to be put in his place. I will pray they find your amazing dog. G'night." He exited the building.

Howie returned with meds and a bottle of water, which he handed to Jayla.

She popped the pills into her mouth and took a drink. "Well, that was interesting. Thank you for your defense, Ranger."

"Anytime. How dare he act like that. Gives other troopers a bad name, just like Gabby—" He stopped.

Jayla shifted in her chair. "Who's Gabby?"

"Doesn't matter." He turned to Howie. "Obviously, we're not going anywhere tonight. You have blankets and pillows?"

"Of course. I'll be staying, too. My home is too far away to get there in this weather. I'll be right back." Howie left the chalet's living room area.

"Sorry for the strange accommodations. This ski area only houses the chalet building." Bryson got up and stoked the fire, adding another log. "At least we'll be warm."

Jayla fished her cell phone out of her pocket. "I need to text Grant and update him. I'm not going back to Canada without Herc."

She pictured her handsome dog's face as a chill slivered through her body despite the warmth from the roaring fire.

Lord, protect Hercules. Wherever he is. Keep him out of the cold and help us to find him.

She couldn't lose the one constant support she had in her life right now.

THIRTEEN

The scent of coffee brewing jolted Jayla from frustrating dreams of failing to rescue Herc from a masked bandit. Heaviness sat on Jayla's chest, lingering like a terrible cold. She threw off the plush green-and-navy-plaid blanket and stood. Her dog was alone and needed her. She checked the time on her cell phone. Seven thirty. Darkness still enveloped the ski chalet. Daylight would arrive soon, but Jayla had to get searching. She couldn't wait any longer. She stretched and observed Bryson, who was still sound asleep on his couch on the other side of the room. His snoring made her snicker, and the idea of throwing a pillow at him emerged. Dare she?

She required something to lighten her load of late, so she picked up her pillow and chucked it at him.

He grunted and launched upright. "What's—"

"Wake up, sleepyhead, and stop snoring."

He smirked. "I do not snore."

Howie entered the room, carrying a pot of coffee. "Oh yes, you do." He laughed and put the carafe on a warming pad in the café area. "Bryson, there's hot water in the kettle. I'm making you both breakfast."

"Awesome." Jayla meandered over to the counter and lifted a mug in Howie's direction. "I need a large caffeine kick this morning. I want to get going."

He poured her a cup. "It's still dark."

Bryson joined her at the walk-up counter, taking a seat on a stool. "Did you sleep at all?"

"As much as I could on a couch. My restless dreams didn't help." She added cream to her coffee and stirred. "I need to find Herc. Now."

He reached over and squeezed her hand. "We will. The search team should arrive soon."

She sipped the cinnamon-flavored coffee. "Howie, would Bertie be up now and have his radio on?"

"Of course. He's an early riser."

Jayla rubbed the back of her head, the reminder of Herc's abduction still fresh. "I want to talk to him."

"I'll get the radio. Just a sec." He left the room.

"I understand your need to get going, but we have to be smart about this." Bryson slid off his stool and stepped behind the counter. He plunked a tea bag into a cup and filled it with hot water.

"Bryson, Herc needs me." How could she explain to him the enormous hole in her heart from being separated from her beloved friend and partner? Her taut chest wouldn't lighten until she held Herc in her arms. Their bond was irreplaceable. "What would you do if—heaven forbid—Avery was taken? My heart is ripped apart right now."

Bryson sighed and put his mug down, then hurried over to her side. He brought her into his arms. "You're right, and I'm sorry. We'll move out after we get in touch with Bertie." He released her but stayed close.

"Thank you." She studied his blue eyes, and her breath hitched. How had this man captured her heart so quickly?

Their gaze locked, and Bryson tucked a strand of hair behind her ear.

Howie bounded into the room and cleared his throat. "Sorry for interrupting." He set the two-way radio in front of Jayla. "He's on the line."

"Thank you." She picked it up and pressed the talk button. "Bertie, this is Jayla Hoyt."

"Howdy, miss. Howie explained your quandary. Unfortunately, I ain't seen hide nor hair of any folks in my area. Mya here would have barked her head off. She's a feisty one, that girl." The man snorted.

Jayla's shoulders sagged. "Sir, is Mya good at tracking animals?"

"How do you think I live out here in the wild? She's the best. Well, her and Rudy."

"Rudy?" Jayla asked.

"My Remington 870, miss."

Jayla stifled a giggle. She already loved this man's "get 'er done" attitude. "Do you think she'd be able to find Hercules if she caught his scent?"

"Doggone it. If Herc's out here, Mya will track 'em."

"Good. Once Howie explains where you are, we'll be there." How much should she tell the man? "Sir, stay safe. There could be dangerous men in your area."

"Don't you worry, young lady. Bertie's as sharp as a tack." Once again, he snorted. "Be careful. Should be light soon, but my achy bones are tellin' me the storm's rearin' its ugly head again."

Great. That's all they needed. "See you soon, sir."

"Roger, dodger. This is Bertie and Mya, over and out."

Bryson puffed out a breath. "Well, he seems like quite the character."

"Wait till you see him." Howie chuckled. "He's a gem, that's for sure. God-fearing man."

"Can you give us his location?" Jayla asked.

"I will—but first, you need a good old-fashioned breakfast to give you energy." Howie walked back to the kitchen.

After a meal of eggs, bacon and hash browns, Howie gave them directions to Bertie's log cabin on Gunrunner

Ridge. Bryson's team along with two troopers had arrived, bringing snowmobiles to help with the search and rescue.

Troopers Nathaniel and Bud agreed to help in the search. Thankfully, Trooper Sanders had declined joining them today, claiming he was too busy. Just as well, Jayla didn't want his bad attitude on the team, especially with Herc's life on the line.

Faith approached Jayla. "Sorry to hear about Herc. We'll find him."

"Thanks." Jayla tucked her jeans into her wool socks and slipped into her snowsuit.

Bryson whistled. "Okay, listen up. We have a wide area to cover." He spread the map out on a table and circled an area. "Faith and Ramsay, you head in this direction." He marked another region. "Troopers Nathaniel and Bud, you go here."

Chris folded his arms. "What about you and Jayla?"

Jayla took the marker from Bryson and circled Gunrunner Ridge. "Here. We want to talk to Bertie." She raised her radio. "Let's keep in constant touch. Make sure we're on the same SAR channel."

"Let's give thirty-minute updates." Bryson turned to the troopers. "Our team has had little activity in these parts. Anything else you can tell us about the terrain?"

"The Elimac Mountain area is rough. Lots of rock, lakes and not much shelter anywhere." Trooper Nathaniel tapped a spot on the map. "However, there's an abandoned ranger station here, if you need it. Not much there any longer, though."

"Our team is aware of all stations. Why not this one?" Bryson asked.

"Hasn't been used in years. They built a new one here." Nathaniel pointed to a spot farther inland.

"Understood." Bryson folded the map and stuffed it into his backpack.

Howie appeared and passed out food supplies to the team. "For energy. This weather will zap it out of you quickly, and I want you to get back here safe and sound."

Jayla smiled. "Thank you. How did you learn to be so kind?"

"My parents taught me well." He stuffed a dog treat into her bag. "Something for Herc when you find him."

Ice pellets clanged against the floor-to-ceiling windows, alerting them to the storm front moving into the region. Time to get the search and rescue mission started.

Jayla walked over and peered outside. Daylight had finally arrived, revealing the messy conditions. The winter weather had been relentless this season, bringing storm after storm. She turned to the team. "We need to move before it gets worse." She bit the inside of her cheek to stabilize her emotions. "Please, help me find Herc."

Trooper Nathaniel brought his balaclava down over his face and pulled up his parka hood. "We will. Let's head out, Bud." The two left the chalet.

Faith and Chris tucked their radios into their protective outer pockets before leaving the building.

Jayla fastened her coat. "Bry, you okay if I pray before we go?" Not that she was totally trusting God right now, but she wanted to give Herc over to Him.

"Of course."

She held Bryson's hands firmly as she bowed her head. "God, please be with Herc, wherever he is. You know how important he is to me. Help us find him quickly and bring him home. Keep us all safe. Amen."

"Amen." Bryson squeezed her hands. "Let's go."

Twenty minutes later, Jayla revved her engine and followed Bryson up a hill near Gunrunner Ridge. She then parked under a tree, shutting off her engine. They would leave their machines and travel on snowshoe, as the area's steepness was too dangerous to ride to the ridge.

Jayla took her snowshoes from the rack and put them on. She opened the map she'd downloaded on her cell phone and enlarged it, comparing their location to where Howie had said Bertie lived. She pointed. "Okay, it's about two miles that way."

"Keep your eyes open. Nathaniel mentioned multiple sharp rocks in this area." He unhooked his radio from his belt. "I'm going to check in with the others before we go any farther."

After talking to the teams and finding out they hadn't spotted any suspicious activity, Bryson and Jayla headed toward the ridge. The ice pellets had turned into a full-blown snowstorm.

Scattered tracks leading to the right of her location caught her eye. "Bryson, someone has been here." She bent low and examined the snowed-over indentations, sucking in a breath. "Dog and human tracks."

He squatted. "Could be Bertie and Mya's."

"Or Herc's."

"Possibly." Bryson pointed to the ridge. "I see smoke rising. We're almost to Bertie's."

They continued toward the log cabin as the blinding blizzard obstructed their journey, but Jayla kept trudging through the deep snow toward Bertie and Mya. She wasn't about to turn around now.

Herc depended on her to rescue him from his abductors.

Bryson's pulse pounded from the excursion up the side of the mountain. The growing burning-wood scent told him they were almost at the cabin. Questions tumbled through his mind as to why someone would live this isolated from the rest of the world. Was Bertie hiding from something? Or was he just that much of a recluse and longed for total privacy? The thought of being secluded had its appeal, but Bryson couldn't stay hidden from everyone and everything forever.

His breathing labored from the higher elevation, so he stopped and sipped his water. *You can do this. Remember what's at stake.* They must find Hercules. Jayla depended on him, and he would not fail her again.

A dog barked in the distance.

Jayla stopped beside him and drank from her thermos. "That must be Mya." She paused. "Yup, it's not Herc's bark. We're almost there."

"Why would anyone live in such a remote place?"

"Good question." She tucked her thermos away.

Bryson stuffed his bottle into his backpack. "Let's keep going."

Ten minutes later, the log cabin came into view. The rustic structure reminded Bryson of something they'd see in a movie. A small cabin with a front veranda and a rocking chair beside the door. Woodpile off to the side, along with a chopping block and an axe propped against it.

Intensified barking sounded from inside the cabin, telling Bryson no one could creep up on this mountain man. Not with Mya keeping watch.

The door creaked open, and a tall, burly man with a salt-and-pepper beard that kissed the top of his protruding belly tramped onto the porch. Dressed in an open fur-lined hooded parka, ball cap, overalls and a blue-and-black-plaid shirt, the man personified everything Bryson ever thought a recluse living on a mountain would look like.

He turned to study Jayla's expression and forced himself not to laugh. Her mouth hung open, and her widened eyes revealed her shock. Even though Howie had warned them.

A hound dog shot out from the entrance and bounded down the steps, barking and baring her teeth.

"Mya! Stop. Company's here." Bertie tucked his thumbs into the straps of his overalls. "Howdy, folks." He walked down the steps and held out his hand to Jayla. "You, purdy lady, must be Jayla."

Her shocked expression turned into a radiant smile. "I am. Nice to meet you, Bertie." She gestured toward Bryson. "This is Alaska State park ranger Bryson Clarke."

They shook hands.

"Nice to meet y'all." Bertie pointed to his dog. "This critter is my Mya."

She barked.

Jayla squatted and patted the dog. "Sure hope you can help find my Herc, Mya."

"Little lady, I reckon if Herc's in my woods, Mya will help find him."

"Sir, have you seen anything questionable in your area?" Bryson asked.

"Call me Bertie." He tapped his knobby index finger on his bearded chin. "Now that ya mention it, I thought I'd seen some city slickers over yonder on Elimac Mountain when wees was a' huntin'."

"What were they doing?" Jayla took off her backpack, setting it on the ground.

"Lugging some tools in a sled." Bertie pushed his ball cap tighter on his head. "Thought it odd at the time, but forgot after Mya went chasing after a hare."

Bryson guessed it was probably near the cave they'd found. "When was this?"

"A week past."

The time frame fit with the avalanche and their discovery. "Anything else, Bertie? How about since last night, early evening? That's when someone abducted Hercules."

"Plus, we found tracks on our way here," Jayla said.

Bertie's eyes widened. "Well, I best get Rudy, then. You wanna come inside and warm up?"

"We're good." Jayla opened her bag. "We want to get searching, if that's okay."

"Sure is." He raced back into the cabin and came out seconds later with a backpack, raising his Remington. "If there be hooligans in my woods, they won't get past me."

Bryson raised his hands. "Bertie, please—if you see any of these assailants, please contact the police. Don't take matters into your own hands. They're dangerous."

The man harrumphed. "No lawman has been in these parts. Not since I've lived here. I need to protect my woods."

"I'm curious. Why do you live so secluded and shut off from the world?" Bryson couldn't contain his question. Not that it was any of his business, but he still wanted to know.

Bertie stared into the distance, his wrenched expression revealing his pain. "Because the world stole my love."

Jayla reached out and squeezed his arm. "I'm so sorry. How did she die?"

"Murdered. She was a lawyer who put away a city slicker. I failed her." He turned his gaze back to Bryson. "I was a lawman once but still couldn't stop 'em from murdering my wife after a fellow officer betrayed me and gave away our location."

No wonder he felt the need to live off the grid. Betrayed by one of his own—something Bryson had learned from experience. "I'm sorry to hear that. I can relate."

Jayla turned to Bryson with an inquisitive look on her face.

Oops. Now he'd have to tell her more, but was he ready to share that dark hole of his life?

Bertie checked his shotgun. "Now it's just me, Mya and the good ole Lord up here, and I'm fine with that."

Bryson's radio squawked.

"Clarke, nothing to report," Ramsay said. "Faith and I are retreating to the chalet. So are the troopers. You need to come back, too. We can't find anything in this weather."

Bryson glanced at Jayla.

Her lips pressed into a firm line, and she shook her head. "I'm not leaving this mountain without Herc."

Bryson wanted to argue that they didn't even know if Hercules was still in the region, but he remained silent and nodded. He wouldn't give up either. "We're with Bertie here, and about to get Mya to search. We'll report if we find anything."

"Suit yourself. I'm not risking my life for a dog." Ramsay's tone held disdain.

"Doggone varmint. He's got 'imself a stinker of an attitude." Bertie zippered up his parka. "He's right about the storm, though. I reckon we need to find Herc before the mountain gets angrier. You got something Mya can get a scent from, purdy lady?"

"I do." Jayla dug into her knapsack and withdrew Hercules's toy. She handed it to the man. "I'll let you do your thing. I know the bond between a dog and their handler."

The man took the tug ball and squatted in front of his dog, holding the toy in front of her nose. "Mya, girl. Time to work. Smell this."

Mya sniffed.

"Mya, seek." Bertie handed the ball back to Jayla. "Now we watch her to see if she gets a scent in this nasty weather."

Mya raised her snout in the air, then barked seconds later and dashed toward the trees.

Bertie put on his pack and raised his shotgun. "She's a' trackin'. Let's follow."

Bryson and Jayla grabbed their bags, scurrying after the mountain man and his dog. Hope flushed through Bryson's body. Maybe this day would end better than yesterday.

He picked up speed and trudged faster through the snowstorm, his purpose of saving her dog steady on his mind.

He'd get Hercules away from the assailants.

He would not fail Jayla this time.

* * *

Jayla wiped the blinding snow from her goggles and followed the duo. The dog had shot off like a dart, which told Jayla that Herc had to be close. But how had the assailants stayed under the mountain man's keen radar?

Her heartbeat echoed in her ears as she struggled to keep up with them. They stumbled down the steep slope they'd just climbed thirty minutes ago, dodging the jagged rocks. Her head throbbed, but she didn't have time to tend to herself. Herc required her protection.

At the bottom of the incline, Mya stopped and once again sniffed the air. Had she lost Herc's scent?

Please, Lord, help her find it again.

Seconds later, she bounded toward the tree line.

"Mya's gettin' close," Bertie said. "Come on."

Once again, they plowed through the snow and followed the dog's smart tracking nose into the woods.

A bark sounded.

Jayla stopped, holding up her fisted hand as the rhythm in her pounding head increased. "Wait… Listen."

The group paused.

Another bark came from the direction Mya had fled.

"That's Herc!" Jayla gathered strength and willed her shaky legs to move faster.

Within minutes, they found Mya sitting in front of a group of trees. A hint of golden brown flashed from behind the snow-covered branches before Herc emerged, barked and touched noses with the other dog.

Mya had found Jayla's beloved friend.

"Hercules, come!" Jayla broke into a run. *Thank You, Lord, for bringing us to Herc. Please help him be okay.*

Herc turned in their direction, shook off the snow and scampered toward Jayla.

Jayla fell to her knees as Herc met her halfway. "I'm so

glad Mya found you." Tears fogged her goggles, but she ignored them and hugged him harder.

Bryson dropped beside her. "Is he okay?"

Jayla removed her gloves and combed her hands along Herc's body, searching for any type of injury. Nothing. She expelled a long breath. "You're fine, bud. I missed you."

Herc barked.

Mya trotted over to them, and Jayla smothered the pooch with kisses. "Thank you, girl."

"Told ya if Herc was here, Mya'd find 'em." Bertie tossed his dog a treat.

Bryson held out a long, frayed rope hanging from Herc's collar. "Looks like they tied Hercules up, but he escaped." He untied it and stuffed it into his backpack.

Jayla once again felt her dog's body. "He's not too chilled, so I'm guessing he may have just broke free from his captors." She shoved her gloves back on.

Bryson stood. "Which means they're probably not far behind." He turned to Bertie. "You and Mya best return to your cabin and lie low. Stat."

Bertie raised his shotgun. "I ain't scared of 'em. Rudy and Mya will keep me safe."

Jayla pushed herself into a standing position. "We need to get back to the chalet before the storm gets worse. We can barely see where we're going now." She rubbed Herc's back. "Plus, I want a vet to check him out. They drugged him, and I have to ensure he's okay."

"Agreed." Bryson held out his hand. "Bertie, thank you for your help. It was a pleasure meeting you and Mya."

They shook hands. "No prob. You're welcome in my neck of the woods anytime."

"Please call the Cross-Border Mountain Task Force if you see anything out of the ordinary, okay?" Bryson dug a card out of his backpack and handed it to him.

"I will." Bertie held out his hand to Jayla. "Goodbye, purdy lady."

Jayla pulled him into a hug. "Thank you for bringing my Herc back to me."

"Gosh, it's my honor. You take care, ya hear?"

"We will." Jayla bent and kissed Mya. "Bye, girl."

Mya barked before darting back the way they'd come.

"Guess she wants to get home." Bertie tipped his parka hood at them in goodbye and followed Mya, humming "Victory in Jesus."

Jayla chuckled and prayed a silent prayer for the mountain man and his dog's safety. "Well, it would've been fun to get to know him a bit better. What an extraordinary person."

"Sure is. I bet there's more to his story than he shared." Bryson pointed in the opposite direction. "Let's go before Hercules's abductors come our way."

Thirty minutes later, they reached the edge of a frozen lake. Jayla tensed at the sound of voices booming from the trees.

"Where did that darned dog get to?" the voice asked. "We best find him, or boss man will have our heads."

Herc growled at the captor's voice.

Jayla yanked him closer to her. They would not get her dog again.

Two men emerged from the tree line and stopped when they spotted them. "There he is!" one of them shouted. He raised his rifle.

"Run!" Bryson yelled, pointing at the lake. "It will get us back to the chalet faster."

They darted onto the ice.

Jayla stole a glimpse over her shoulder. The men were in pursuit.

She tried to gain speed but failed to spot a patch of ice chunks and fell hard onto the pile. She landed on her stomach, knocking the wind out of her. She tried to call out, but the words stuck in her throat.

Bryson kept up his pace.

Jayla gasped for air, trying to regulate her staggered breathing. She stumbled to get to her feet but kept slipping. "Umph!" *Lord, help me get moving.*

Herc stopped and barked.

Multiple shots cracked the ice.

The thunder-like boom echoed throughout the area, sending spikes of terror consuming her body.

"Jayla!"

The men shot more rounds.

The ice splintered apart, and Jayla struggled to move farther away from the crumbling lake.

"Jayla!" Bryson shot in the assailants' direction.

Herc barked and barreled toward her, his intent clear. Rescue his handler.

"Hercules, stop!" Jayla commanded. She couldn't let her beloved friend come any closer.

He ignored her and charged.

Nausea formed and bile soured on her tongue as an overwhelming sense of dread lured her toward the growing crack. Her arms flailed as she grappled at anything to hold on to, but nothing was there.

Her legs slipped into the hole as Bryson yelled. Herc latched onto her hood and tugged backward.

Freezing water slammed into her, enveloping her as a question cannonballed through her horror-stricken mind.

Would she survive another frozen tomb and see them again?

FOURTEEN

"No!" Bryson fired multiple shots at the assailants as he dropped and crawled on the ice toward Jayla. He had to rescue her before Hercules's grip on her hood pulled him into the hole, too. If she went under totally, the freezing water temperatures would soon overpower her body.

Bryson fired again.

A suspect yelled, falling to his knees as he held his leg.

Bryson's shot had met its target.

The other assailant hauled his partner up and wrapped his arm around the wounded man's waist before retreating into the woods.

Bryson holstered his weapon and slithered to the edge of where Hercules clutched his handler. Seeing the dog's strong hold reminded Bryson of the rope in his backpack. He drew it out and wormed his way closer to the two.

Jayla slipped farther into the hole, bringing Hercules closer to the edge.

"Help! Treading. Water." Her faint cry and broken words told him she didn't have long before her energy would fail, and both dog and handler would plunge into the icy waters below.

Her widened eyes revealed her panicked state.

"Jayla, stay calm. Take slow, deep breaths through your closed lips. Do it for me now."

She breathed in and out.

He tied a knot at the end of the rope and threw it to her.

"Okay, grab hold of this, and kick as I pull you out. Can you do that?" He kept his words steady and even to keep her calm.

She nodded and gripped the rope.

"Okay, kick! Hercules, pull!" Praying for strength and for the ice to hold, Bryson pulled with all his might.

She emerged out of her frozen tomb, her retriever at her side.

"Now, roll away from the hole." Bryson shimmied backward, dragging them at the same time.

Once again, she did as he instructed.

She coughed, struggling for breath.

"I've got you. You're okay." Bryson drew her farther away from the hole to ensure their weight wouldn't crack the ice and haul them both under.

The golden retriever snuggled next to Jayla and licked her face.

"Someone is glad you're okay," Bryson said. "Me too."

"Wh-where. Are. Th-they?" Her stammered words revealed her frozen state.

"Gone. I wounded one, so they fled."

Her teeth clattered as her body trembled. "So c-cold."

Bryson had to get her inside somewhere. He examined the area, trying to determine their location. They were too far away from the chalet, and there was no way she'd make it up the mountain to Bertie's. *Think, Bryson. Think.*

Wait. What had Trooper Nathaniel told them earlier about an old station? Bryson wiggled out of his backpack and removed the map. "I have to get you inside." He unfolded it and noted where the trooper had circled, calculating the distance between their current location and the building. One mile.

Too far in her frozen state, but it was their only hope. Would Jayla survive the trek there?

Bryson stuffed the map away and stood. "Jayla, the

abandoned ranger station is closer than the chalet. We need to get there to warm you up and call for help." And to keep them safe from the assailants, but he left that part out. "Can you walk?"

She nodded and tried to push herself up but slipped.

He hooked his arms around her waist and helped her stand. "Lean on me. Let's go. Hercules, come."

Slowly, they hiked to the shoreline and made their way along the edge of the woods.

After fifteen minutes of trudging through the winter conditions, Jayla stumbled. "So. Tired. Need to sit." Her legs buckled, and she fell into the snow.

"Jayla?" He turned her over and checked her vitals.

Steady. She'd fainted.

Bryson gently lifted her into his arms. "We're almost there, beautiful."

Did he just call her beautiful again? Good thing she didn't hear it.

The abandoned log ranger station came into view fifteen minutes later. The tattered structure lay nestled in the woods, miles from anywhere. A hare hopped across the veranda before skirting around back at their intrusion into its secluded world.

Bryson let a breath seethe through his teeth as relief washed over him. *Thank You.* He wasn't sure how much farther he could have walked carrying Jayla.

He gasped as a picture flooded his mind.

A cross-stitch his mother had created shortly after becoming a Christian. The scene had two sets of footprints along an ocean shore, but as they reached the forefront, only one remained. His mother had explained how God carried them through struggles in life.

Is that what You're doing, Lord, as I carry Jayla?

Perhaps his mother was right. Bryson needed to give it

more thought, but right now, his only task was to get them into the station's safety. A question rose.

Would it shelter them from the fierce storm and the assailants skulking somewhere in the woods?

Jayla wrestled in and out of a sleep stupor as her dreams tormented her, taking her into dark places where she struggled to get her head above water. Ice chilled her veins, and waves sucked her into the abyss moments before a hand reached in and yanked her upward. She bolted awake.

Warmth wrapped her in its blanket, and she opened her eyes. Dusk had descended, and a glow filled the tiny room. Where was she? She battled to clear her foggy mind. Nightmares plagued her of the time in her life she had tried hard to forget—locked in her mother's restaurant freezer. The small room had gotten accidentally sealed, and she wasn't rescued for hours. The experience had conditioned her body to cold weather. A positive from a negative experience. However, the panic from that situation had crept into her adult life.

Herc stirred beside her, and she hugged him closer. She'd almost lost him, and she vowed not to let him out of her sight. Images of seeing him and Bryson moments before she fell—

She jerked upward, and a chill shot through her body as she remembered the freezing waters, then Bryson helping her escape her icy grave. She also remembered his arms carrying her through the deep snow. What kind of man would do that for her?

Not the man from the grizzly attack. He *had* changed. She realized that now. Her previous feelings for him—before Julie's attack—had reemerged stronger. And had she heard him call her "beautiful"? Or had she dreamed his words?

She brought the blanket tighter to her neck and inspected the cabin. The glow from the lantern sitting on the coffee table in front of her gave her ample light. A fire crackled in the small hearth. The room was comprised of a broken desk, table and chairs, a galley kitchen, and a living area. At least the rustic, outdated ranger station provided shelter for them—but where was Bryson?

Jayla kissed Herc's forehead. "I'm so glad you're okay, bud. I thought I'd lost you."

Ruff! He licked her face.

She giggled.

The door opened, and Bryson entered with logs in his arms. He stomped off the snow. "You're awake. How are you feeling?"

"Tired. Thanks for saving my life and taking care of me."

Bryson dumped the wood beside the fireplace. "Well, Hercules helped. I was so scared I wouldn't get to you in time with the suspects still shooting at us. How did you get so far behind?"

She stiffened. "I stumbled and fell on chunks of ice, and it knocked the wind out of me, so I couldn't call out. Then they started shooting. Before I knew it, the ice cracked, and I fell in. It all happened so fast." She shivered and cuddled closer to Herc. "Where did the shooters go?"

"I wounded one, so they took off into the woods." He added a log to the fire. "They're probably still out there somewhere, though. After I brought you here, I cleaned the flue and looked for dry wood. Rangers haven't used this place in years, but there was still wood sheltered in a small shed out back."

"Is having a fire safe?"

He pursed his lips. "Probably not. I checked the perimeter and didn't see any tracks following ours before I started it. It's risky to light a fire, but it couldn't be helped. I had to warm you up and raise your body temperature."

"Have you radioed the team?"

"Yes, but they can't get to us in the storm. We have to wait it out." He moved to the table and picked up his backpack. "You hungry? Howie packed us a sandwich."

"Thanks." She stroked Herc. "Did you give him anything yet?"

"Yes, treats from your bag…after I dried them out, of course." He handed her a wrapped sandwich.

"What time is it?" She unwrapped the sandwich and took a bite.

He glanced at his watch. "Six thirty. We've been here for hours. I just finished another perimeter sweep. The storm covered our previous tracks, and I didn't see any others, so we're good. For now." He opened his baggie and stuffed a bite of sandwich into his mouth before plunking down into the rocker.

Jayla studied the man who'd saved her life. Dark shadows under his blue eyes told her he was tired. Probably from having to carry her so far. "Can I ask you a question?"

"Sure. Shoot."

"Why did you freeze when you saw the grizzly in Julie's path? Why not help?" A question she'd wondered about for six long months. She had asked at the time, but he'd refused to give a valid response.

He diverted his gaze to the fireplace.

The dancing flames created a flickering rhythm matching the crackling fire, intruding on the silence.

"I've seen a change in you since then, Bry." She pondered her words. "You're more compassionate and gentle. I'm just still wondering why you didn't act quicker that day. You were closer to the site where Julie was attacked." She clamped her lips tight to stop the pending tears. Her anger toward Bryson lessened, but she still wanted answers.

"I knew the day would come when I had to explain myself. It's just hard to admit my failure." He set aside his half-eaten sandwich. "I should have told you earlier, but guilt over my actions silenced me. Guilt not only from Julie's attack but my sister's."

"What do you mean?"

"My sister just lost her husband a few months prior, and I was trying to help bring her and Avery's lives back to some sort of normalcy, so I insisted on a camping trip. Our family loved to camp when we were kids, and Ellie always said it relaxed her. So I thought it would help. She agreed—albeit reluctantly."

"What happened?" Jayla drew her knees to her chest and wrapped her arms around them.

"I woke early that morning and decided to go fishing. Wanted to surprise them with a treat for supper. On my way back to the site, I heard Ellie scream. I dropped my catch and ran. What I discovered rocked my world. A grizzly had stalked Avery and charged in her direction when Ellie screamed to get its attention."

Realization hit her hard. No wonder he'd froze at Julie's attack. It had thrust him to that point in time. "What happened?"

Bryson leaned backward, resting his head against the rocker. "I can still see it when I close my eyes. Ellie dove in front of her daughter to protect her. I tried to intervene, but I was too late. The beast—" He stopped.

"You don't have to go on. I get it. I'm so sorry."

He got up and sat beside her on the couch. "I need to explain. That was the day my fear of bears consumed me, along with the guilt of letting it happen."

"But it wasn't your fault."

He hissed a breath through his teeth. "It was, according to my father. He blamed me for insisting I take Ellie and Avery on the camping trip. I put them in harm's way."

She took his hands in hers. "He's wrong. You were only trying to help by giving them a ray of hope in their world."

Something passed over his handsome face too quickly for her to get a read on the emotion.

Regret? More guilt?

Guilt… Something she, too, struggled with every day. If only—

Don't go there.

"I understand now why you froze at Julie's attack. It brought back painful memories of Ellie."

He tore his hands away and stood, moving to the window. He peered into the darkness. "I thought I'd dealt with the pain, but the scene stopped me in my tracks. I'm so sorry, Jay. Julie is in a wheelchair because of me."

Hearing his side of what happened brought everything into perspective. She'd been wrong to blame him, just like his father was wrong to blame him for Ellie's death. She pushed the blanket off and walked over to his side, placing her hand on his back.

He turned and looked into her eyes.

A small inhale escaped as the emotion radiating on his face consumed her. She stepped backward. She couldn't go there. Not after Michael.

She cleared her throat. "Bryson, I was wrong about you. I see that now. It wasn't your fault. It was the grizzly's." She paused before adding, "At Julie's attack and Ellie's."

"I knew after Julie's injury I hadn't dealt with everything as best as I thought, so I decided on more counseling." He sighed. "However, sometimes the guilt returns. But one person helps me through. Avery."

His expression softened at the mention of his niece's name.

"I can tell you're doing an amazing job parenting her. She's adorable."

"She's the best and like a daughter to me. I applied to adopt her several months ago, but I'm waiting on the courts." Bryson walked back to the rocking chair and picked up the other half of his sandwich. "Tell me something, since we're getting personal... You know my fear. What's yours?"

Jayla plopped down on the couch and rubbed Herc's belly. "What makes you think I have one?"

He scrunched his face. "Everybody has some type of fear."

Jayla pictured the darkened freezing room and shuddered. She covered her shoulders with the blanket to ward off the memory and the sudden chill.

"See, told you. I can tell by the look on your face. What is it?"

"Tight spaces. That's part of the reason I fainted after you pulled me from the lake." She collected her thoughts. "My mother used to own a small restaurant, and one day after school, I went there to wait for her to close up. I wandered into their freezer to get some ice cream. While in there, I tried to get something on the top shelf, but I fell backwards and hit my head. Knocked me unconscious. My mom thought I'd gone home, so she locked the freezer like normal and left."

"What happened?"

"When she realized I wasn't at the house, she came back and found me. Hours later."

"So now you're scared of small places."

She rubbed her hands together to warm them. "Yup, and being buried."

"And yet you're a mountain-survival specialist, and you help find people buried in the snow. Kind of ironic."

"Right? Being in the freezer also made my body somewhat conditioned to the cold. Plus, I've always loved the mountains. My experience instilled in me a desire to help find people." She nestled in closer to Herc. "And this guy makes it all worthwhile."

"Why did you go into the military, then?"

Jayla bristled as her stomach knotted. She wasn't ready to talk about her army experience.

She lay back down and covered herself with the blanket. "I'm tired and need rest."

She closed her eyes, but not before she spotted his pained, tangled-up expression.

Stupid, Jay. You closed the door and snuffed out any opportunity to develop a relationship with the man.

However, it was for the best.

She couldn't let her heart be broken ever again.

Hours later, Bryson stared at the cabin's ceiling and tried to get comfortable on the rickety rocking chair as he thought back to the abrupt end to what he'd perceived as a friendly conversation. They'd both shared information from their pasts, but for some odd reason, something from Jayla's military experience troubled her. He'd read it on her contorted face when he asked the question. She was keeping it a secret.

Just like you. You didn't tell her the entire reason for your counseling.

The wind howled outside the cabin and seeped through the aged timber walls. He got up and tightened the blanket around Jayla, studying her face. *You are beautiful.* Her exquisite features had awakened something inside him he thought he'd locked down as tight as Fort Knox. He couldn't deny his growing feelings for the woman asleep on the couch. Images of Gabby filled his mind. Images he wished he could erase, but her betrayal hit too hard.

No, Bryson would curtail any further feelings from developing. His and Avery's hearts were at risk.

He sat back down and pulled his parka closer to block out the cold. The chill was probably for the best since he'd promised Jayla he would keep watch for any suspicious activity.

A noise jolted Bryson from a restless snooze. *Stupid! You fell asleep.* He popped upright in the seat and listened. What had he heard? He read the time on his watch. 4:00 a.m.

Ruff!

Herc's muffled bark told him the dog had heard it, too. Bryson eased out of the rocker and tiptoed to the window.

Flashlight beams bounced among the trees near the cabin. Bryson's muscles contracted.

They'd found them. How? Only their team knew their location. Someone had betrayed them.

He hurried to Jayla's side and gently shook her. "Jayla, wake up. We have to leave. Now."

She gasped and sat up. "What's happening?"

"Someone is outside." He helped her stand. "We'll sneak out the back."

"But where will we go?"

Good question.

He stuffed his balaclava over his face, drawing up his hood. "Wait. I remember noticing a service road a mile or two from this station. I need to call for help."

"But I thought they couldn't get to us. Who would you call? Someone from our team has obviously leaked our location."

"Other than you, I trust only one person to keep us safe." He stuffed on his gloves.

"Who?"

"My dad." He switched the radio channel to one he knew his father would be on. "Lieutenant Clarke, do you read?"

He waited.

No response. *Come on, Dad. I know you keep your radio on at all times.* "Lieutenant Clarke, Sockeye needs help. Do you read?"

"What does that mean?" Jayla asked.

"While we were on a salmon-fishing trip, we were having fun talking about spy stories, so we made up the secret 'I need help, come and get me' 911 code phrase."

"When was this?"

"Long before our relationship soured. Hopefully, he hasn't forgotten it." He pressed the talk button again. "Lieutenant, Sockeye needs help."

"Read you, Sockeye." His father's groggy voice sailed through the radio. "Report."

"Extract from the northwest Elimac ranger–station service road." Bryson prayed no one else was listening to the outdated channel.

"ETA is sixty minutes. Lie low."

Bryson understood their location was not just around his father's corner. "Can't. Compromised. On the run. Will light the beacon and take cover."

"Understood."

Hercules barked and raced toward the front door.

The assailants were getting closer.

Bryson grabbed Jayla and nudged her away from the front of the station. "Hurry, Lieutenant!"

"En route. Stay safe."

Bryson tucked the radio into his pocket and secured his backpack on his shoulders. "We need a diversion to escape."

Jayla looked around. "Are there any type of weapons left in this old cabin?"

"None that will—" He stopped as an idea formed. "When we first got here, I found some old supplies in the kitchen cabinet. Just not sure how long they've been here."

"Like what?"

"Gasoline, rags and old wine bottles."

She sucked in a breath. "To make a Molotov cocktail?"

"Probably a couple. We can throw them out the window and create a smoke screen. The snow will probably sizzle it out quickly, but it should be enough of a distraction." He yanked her sleeve. "Get Hercules and head into the kitchen. We need to move quickly."

After rushing to make two cocktails, Bryson peeked out the window to get a read on the assailants' location.

A flashlight beam by a tree a few yards away went out.

Gunfire erupted, peppering the front entrance.

Bryson ducked and turned to Jayla. "You ready?"

She nodded.

Bryson threw open the window and chucked the lit cocktails onto the snow-covered veranda.

The explosion ignited a small fire and smoke screen, shielding their movements.

More gunfire exploded.

"Go!" Bryson pushed her toward the back entrance.

"Hercules, come!" Jayla whispered.

They exited through the door as a wind gust smothered Bryson's breath and reminded him of the perilous conditions they faced.

On the run in the middle of a snowstorm with suspects at their heels.

If he was going to place his trust in God, now would be the time.

Lord, bring Dad quickly.

FIFTEEN

Jayla stumbled through the door, following Herc and Bryson. She turned to check the cabin's status. Smoke rose from the front, and the sound of gunfire continued. Their ruse had worked. The suspects still thought they were inside, but how long before they discovered the truth? She prayed the fire they'd started would sizzle out in the snowstorm.

After running through the heavy snow for ten minutes, Jayla's breath wavered as her heart rate quickened. Were they far enough away? "Bryson. Need. To. Stop." She kept her voice low.

Bryson stopped. "You okay?"

"Just need to catch my breath. That freezing water took out more of me than I thought. Where are we?" She inhaled and exhaled deeply, trying to slow her erratic pulse.

Herc nudged her legs, as if reassuring his handler he was there for her. She reached down and petted his head.

"I don't want to turn the flashlight on yet," Bryson said.

She slumped against a tree trunk. "Where can we hide? These trees won't shelter us for long once they see we're not in the cabin." Plus, what animals lurked in the wilderness?

"Once we get to the service road, we'll be more accessible to my dad. However, he won't be here for an hour or more. Ideas on how to stay hidden and warm?"

Jayla racked her foggy, tired brain for a solution to their

current predicament. What would she tell her trainees? *Think, Jayla.*

Once again, Herc nudged her.

His presence reminded her of a trick she'd told a group of rookie police officers. "I got it. We dig a hole and then cover ourselves with tree branches to stay hidden until your dad arrives. The hole will also shelter us from the wind." She tugged on his arm. "Yes, it sounds crazy, but do you have any other ideas?"

"No. We need to get to the road first and then wait for him to give our secret whistle signal we also cooked up on that same fishing trip."

Jayla smiled. Sounded like something a son and father would do. "Did you turn the beacon on?" Jayla asked.

Bryson turned. "It's in my backpack. Can you get it?"

Jayla fished it out and flipped on the device. "Done. Let's go."

After walking for another twenty minutes and turning the flashlight on at intervals, they found the road. With no further sightings of anyone following them, they cut several thick tree branches and started digging. Once their fort was deep enough, they sheltered themselves inside and hauled the branches overtop to conceal them completely.

Voices sounded from outside their cocoon sometime later. Jayla had no sense of time in their hiding place. She waited for the signal.

A bird call echoed throughout the forest.

Bryson answered using the same call. "That's Dad." He pushed off the branches, and they crawled out of their hiding place. A bouncing flashlight beam headed in their direction.

Lieutenant Trent Clarke approached. "You guys okay?"

His concern for his son was evident by his knotted expression.

"Cold, but fine." Bryson brushed snow from his jacket. "Let's get out of here before the suspects find us."

Two hours later, Jayla sat huddled on the Clarkes' comfy couch, nursing a cup of hazelnut coffee while Bryson explained to his parents everything that had happened on the mountain pass.

Lieutenant Clarke sprang from his chair. "Son, you can't keep this a secret any longer. Bring your team in on it."

Herc lifted his head. The man's rough voice must have stirred him from where he'd been sleeping beside her. Jayla rubbed his back. "It's okay, bud. Go back to sleep."

Bryson raked his fingers through his wavy hair. "I'm not sure who to trust. Someone is leaking information, as Murdoc keeps finding us no matter what precautions we take."

"By not sharing information, you're putting all of their lives at risk." He pointed to Jayla. "Her building was buried, and I'm pretty sure the avalanche that did it was not an accident, from what you're saying. Sergeant Park can be rough around the edges, but he's trustworthy."

"He's right, Bryson." Jayla set her mug on the coffee table. "I've known Sergeant Park and Kerry for two years. Grant is like a father to me. We can trust him. I'm tired of running. We need help to bring Murdoc down."

Bryson flattened his lips.

The look on his handsome face told her he didn't like Jayla siding with his father.

But it couldn't be helped.

Shannon sat beside her son, taking his hand in hers. "I agree. Stop trying to be the hero I know you already are."

"Fine. Let's set up a joint task meeting in Carimoose Bay, Jayla." He stood. "I'll call Supervisor Thamesford."

"I want to attend to represent the state troopers. I realize some of my men help on your team." Trent rubbed his temple. "Plus, I need to monitor you both. I don't like that this Murdoc person is targeting you."

"Fine." Bryson turned to his mother. "Mom, did you hear anything more from your Canadian contact about an illegal copper-mining ring in the Yukon?"

She jumped to her feet. "Yes, just a sec." She left the room and then returned, carrying her tablet. She set it on the coffee table in front of them. "Okay, here's where the known copper mines are situated or at least were at one time. Some have closed." She enlarged the map and pointed to various sites around the Whitehorse area. "Zoe told me none are registered on the Ogilwyn Mountain Pass, so her boss is sending her to scope it out."

The hairs on Jayla's neck prickled. "Is that wise? Murdoc has proven to be dangerous. We need to let the authorities do that."

"Let's get your constables on it," Bryson said. "Mom, when are they sending her?"

"In two days. She's at a conference right now."

Jayla fished out her cell phone. "Then let's make our meeting in two days and invite Zoe. She needs to know the potential danger she might walk into. I'll get Sergeant Park to get one of his constables to go with her. Speaking of him, I need to give him an update. He'll be worried sick."

"I'll talk to Thamesford, and then we'll head to Carimoose Bay." Bryson left the room.

Jayla reached down and rubbed Herc's head. "We're going home, bud."

Her cell phone chimed before she could make her call. She swiped the screen.

Park Ranger Clarke can't keep you safe. M

Jayla bristled. "M" for Murdoc. Why had he waited until now to contact her, and how did he get her number? It told Jayla one thing. He was nervous.

They were getting close to discovering his identity and stopping his mining ring.

Two days later, Bryson stood at the front of Carimoose Bay's municipal town boardroom, ready to make their presentation to the entire Cross-Border Mountain Task Force. Since the avalanche had demolished Jayla's station, it was the only spot large enough to house the CBM team and guests. His mother's friend Zoe sat beside Bryson's father. His powerful presence both intimidated and comforted Bryson—if that was even possible. However, Supervisor Leon Thamesford's glare revealed the man's disdain for Bryson calling this meeting. When Bryson had mentioned it to his leader, he hesitated at the idea and would not do it until Lieutenant Clarke put his foot down. It was clear the two men didn't get along.

Supervisor Thamesford reported that local authorities hadn't discovered any prints on the tracking device they'd found on the crashed helicopter. Not that Bryson had expected they would.

Bryson smoothed out his ranger uniform and observed the woman beside him. The two days had given her much-needed rest, and her steeled jaw hinted that she was ready to end this danger and catch Murdoc. She'd shared the text she'd received, and her constables had tried to determine its origin but were unsuccessful.

"Dana, where's Joshua?" Jayla asked.

"On leave. His father just passed away." The constable leaned closer. "He wanted me to tell you that he's sorry for the way he acted the other day. He's been sick with worry over this family situation."

"That explains it. Thanks for letting me know." Jayla cleared her throat. "Let's get started. We have lots to cover in a short time. Ranger Clarke will brief you on his discovery of mysterious avalanches in our joint mountain pass."

Bryson clicked the remote, and several documents appeared on the screen. "Over the past two months, the weather conditions haven't warranted the avalanches they've supposedly caused. So I looked into it closer and detected some anomalies. Plus, we found this at the site where Ethan was killed." He clicked the button, and an image of the blasting cap appeared.

After taking the team through the events from the past few days and sharing about Murdoc, including his possible copper-mining ring, Bryson addressed Jayla. "Anything to add?"

"Just that Murdoc seems to know our every move, so please be careful." Jayla walked around the table. "Questions?"

"You're saying they're mining for copper ore in our mountains in the winter?" Ramsay huffed. "Doesn't seem possible."

"We don't have all the details yet." Bryson changed the screen to reveal the pictures they'd taken. "But our geologist confirmed this is copper ore, and this cave was on Elimac Mountain, right at the Alaskan–Yukon border."

"You mean *your mother* confirmed it?" Ramsay folded his arms, tilting his head. "She probably told you that to confirm your bizarre theory so you'd get a promotion."

Bryson's father slammed his hand down. "I can assure you my wife knows what she's talking about, young man."

Ramsay uncrossed his arms. "I don't believe this for one minute. These avalanches aren't man-made."

Bryson suppressed the anger bubbling to the surface and placed his hands on the table, leaning forward. "How do you explain us getting shot at, Hercules being abducted and the other tragedies?"

"Part of your scheme to rise to the top," Ramsay said.

Supervisor Thamesford slammed his hard-cover note-book shut, the sound resonating. "Ramsay, enough. You're being unprofessional and I won't tolerate your behavior. We assume this is what's happening. Clarke's right—we've had too many deaths to deny something's going on."

Sergeant Park turned his cell phone over and waggled his finger at Ramsay. "This madman killed my son. You need to lay off." He turned to Zoe. "Can you confirm the assessment of this rock?"

"I can. That's definitely copper ore, sir." She addressed Ramsay. "I've seen enough to identify it. I can also confirm there are no mines registered in this region, so they're hiding their discoveries."

Ramsay slouched in his chair.

Bryson dug his nails into his palms to curb his frustration over this man's animosity toward him. What had he done to deserve it?

Sergeant Park's phone buzzed and vibrated on the table, indicating an incoming call. He picked it up. "Park here." A pause. "Are you sure?" Another pause. "I'll get a team there pronto."

He stood. "Jayla, you need to get a team to the base of Augstone Mountain. Lost skier. Friend claims men coming out of a cave chased them, and his skier friend fell over the embankment."

Zoe popped to her feet. "I'm coming, too. Perhaps the cave is one where they're mining for copper."

Supervisor Thamesford stood. "Ramsay, you go with them in case they need a medic. The rest of you need to get back to Faircord Junction. Let's dig deeper into this possible illegal mining ring."

Ugh. Bryson understood why Thamesford was sending

Ramsay, but he didn't have to like it. Working with the man lately had zapped Bryson's energy.

After racing to Augstone Mountain, Bryson parked his snowmobile beside Ramsay and drew him aside. Time to get the man on board. Their conflict affected the team. "Listen, buddy. I don't know what I did to you, but can we please work together? Lives are at stake."

Ramsay stepped closer. "Fine. Just stay away from Faith."

What? Bryson stumbled backward. "What does that mean?"

"Don't you get it? She's crushing on you."

Bryson had a light bulb moment. Ramsay liked the cute rookie ranger himself. "I can assure you, I have no romantic interest in Faith." He glanced at Jayla as she dismounted and Herc hopped down. She fastened on her skis. He turned back to Ramsay. "Now, let's find the skier, shall we?"

Bryson, Ramsay, Zoe, Jayla and Constable Spokene gathered around the skier who'd reported his missing friend.

"Sir, what's your name?" Bryson asked.

"Ian. Can you please find Aaron? He's my best buddy." The man's voice shook.

Jayla reached over to squeeze his arm. "We will. Can you tell us what happened and where you last saw Aaron?"

"We just reached the bottom here when these men appeared out of nowhere."

"How many men?" Constable Spokene asked.

"Two. One carried a shovel and pick. The other had what looked like a box of dynamite in his hands. When they spotted us, they pulled a gun." Emotion contorted his face. "We took off, but Aaron missed a protruding rock and skied into it, then tumbled over the side hill. I skied in his direction but couldn't find him. That's when I called your team. I hear you're the best."

Jayla bent down in front of her dog. "Hercules, search!"

The dog bolted. Jayla followed, skiing after him.

"Ian, can you show Constable Spokene exactly where these men came from?" Bryson asked.

He nodded.

"Dana, take Zoe." He inched closer to the constable. "Be careful. Murdoc is out there somewhere. Radio us when you find something."

Once again, in record time, Hercules found the skier alive. Aaron had hit his head and fallen unconscious in a pile of snow, but Ramsay brought him around. The medic would take him to the hospital to be thoroughly examined. They left with Ian after he'd shown them the spot where they'd seen the men.

Jayla tossed the K-9 his ball. "Good boy."

"Ranger Clarke, we found the cave," Constable Spokene said through the radio. "Head north of your location. You'll see us."

"We're on our way," Bryson said.

They parked their snowmobiles beside Spokene's a few minutes later. Spokene and Zoe stood at the mouth of a small hole.

"Discover anything?" Bryson asked as they approached.

Spokene nodded. "Zoe will take you through what we found. I need to grab something from my machine. Be right back."

"This is unbelievable," Zoe said. "Come and look." She ducked and entered the cave.

Bryson retrieved his flashlight and guided Jayla and Hercules inside.

Damp air assaulted Bryson's nose, but he ignored it and wandered farther into the dark cavern, shining the light around. "This is the same as the other cave we found." He turned to Zoe. "Copper ore?"

"You got it." She lit a lantern sitting on a box. A soft glow filled the tight space, revealing equipment leaning against one stone wall. "I'm guessing they took rock samples using the picks and shovels. Maybe they're marking the caves they want to mine later in the warmer seasons. I need to get a team here to do more investigation."

"I'm not sure it's safe. You'll need a police escort." Bryson pointed to a box of dynamite and firearms.

"I can help." Spokene entered. "Let's head back down the mountain and make arrangements."

"Sounds good." Zoe snapped a few pictures. "We have to stop this gang. How many other caves do you know about?"

Jayla guided her fingers along the damp rocks. "At least two—one other on Ogilwyn Pass and the one on Elimac Mountain." She turned. "Wait. Bryson, why didn't the two men blow the cave like they did the others?"

"Not sure. Maybe they thought the two skiers wouldn't survive the fall." He bent down beside the box of firearms and pulled one out, inspecting it. "They filed the serial numbers off."

Spokene gestured to Zoe. "Let's go."

The pair left. Seconds later, an engine roared to life and dissipated into the distance.

"Look around for anything that can help identify Murdoc." Bryson rummaged through the equipment.

"What's this?" Jayla bent down, shining her light.

A file folder stuck out from under the box of dynamite. She pulled it out and opened it. "Looks like they forgot something."

"What's in there?"

"An invoice. Okay, who issues paperwork for illegal

contraband? Says it's sold to Warblow Brothers Corporation out of Whitehorse." She took a picture of it before placing it back in the folder, then lifted out a map. "They circled multiple locations in red. Zoe's right—they're marking the caves. This is a viable lead. Let's research these brothers." She snapped a photo of the map.

"They're getting sloppy, leaving this behind. It could lead us to Murdoc."

"We can only hope." She leaned against the wall. "We need a break. They killed Ethan."

Bryson caught the quiver in her voice and walked over to her. "You okay?"

"I'm tired and want this to end."

Their gazes locked in the dimly lit cave.

Bryson's heartbeat quickened at their closeness as his emotions for this woman invaded his resolve to stay strong. He couldn't deny his feelings any longer. He eyed her lips and inched closer. "Jayla, I—"

His radio crackled, followed by fragmented words, breaking the intimate moment.

She pushed on his chest, distancing herself. "Hercules, come." She rushed outside with the dog at her heels.

Bryson's posture slumped. *She doesn't feel the same way, Bry. Give it up.*

He pressed the talk button. "Come again?"

Static hissed between broken words.

"I didn't get that." The cave was interfering with the radio waves. He stepped outside. "Say again."

"Ranger Clarke. You're proving to be a nuisance," the distorted voice said. "So I've taken matters into my own hands."

Bryson straightened. What did that mean? "Who's this?"

Jayla turned at his question and quirked a brow before hurrying to his side.

"Can't you guess? It's Murdoc."

Hercules ran toward the tree line, barking.

Something had the dog rattled.

Trepidation swept through Bryson. "How did you get this channel?"

"Not important. What is important is who's here beside me. Talk, little girl."

"Uncle Bry?"

Jayla clutched his arm at the sound of his niece's voice.

Pain tightened Bryson's chest as terror weakened his knees. "Avery?"

"When are you—"

"That's enough," Murdoc said. "Ranger Clarke, here's the deal. You, Jayla and Hercules are to come to Alaska alone to the coordinates I'm about to give you. Bring all the evidence you have. Then you can have sweet Avery back." He rattled off the latitude and longitude. "Got that, or do I need to repeat myself?"

Bryson gripped the radio tighter and hissed through his teeth. "Got it. Do. Not. Hurt. Her."

"You play by the rules and I won't. Remember, tell no one. Oh, and have fun getting here." The radio went silent.

"What does that mean?" Bryson dropped to his knees, holding his head in his hands. Guilt reemerged at the thought of not being able to protect his sister's child. "I can't lose her."

Jayla wrapped her arms around him. "We'll find her. I promise."

Hercules's barking increased.

Bryson flinched and pulled away. From the time they'd spent together, the dog hadn't barked that much unless it was for a reason. "Does he see someone in the trees?" Bryson unholstered his weapon, moving toward Hercules.

Jayla followed. "What is it, bud?"

An explosion rocked both snowmobiles, sending fiery shrapnel flying.

Bryson grabbed Jayla and dove to the ground. His chest constricted as grief twisted his broken heart.

How would Bryson get off the mountain to rescue his sweet niece?

SIXTEEN

Jayla lay flat in the snow, waiting for the buzzing in her brain to still. Seconds after the explosion, she had latched onto Herc and vaulted away from the blast's trajectory, narrowly missing pieces. She scrambled to her feet, regretting the quick response as her world spun and spots twinkled in her vision. She closed her eyes and prayed for the dizziness to pass. "Bryson! You okay?"

He moaned.

She opened her eyes and hurried forward, dropping into the snow by his side. "Where are you hurt?"

Herc nestled beside the ranger and licked his face, as if trying to help.

He held his arm. "I think a piece of shrapnel may have sliced through my coat."

"Let me look." Jayla gently moved his arm. "Yup, there's a cut there, and you're bleeding. We need to get help."

He eased himself into a seated position and wiggled out of his sleeve, examining the injury. "Surface wound. I'll be fine. We have to get off the mountain. Avery needs me." Bryson hugged Herc. "If it wasn't for this guy, I'm afraid we may not have survived that blast. He brought us away from the snowmobiles."

Jayla scanned the machine parts strewn across the snow along with their broken skis. "How did Murdoc access our snowmobiles?"

"I've been asking myself that same question. Did someone sabotage them while we were looking for the skier?"

"You think this could have been Dana or Chris? No way." She bit her lip. "Dana's a sweetheart. Chris is rough around the edges—but is he capable of something like this?"

"Honestly, I'm not sure. I figured out why he's been acting strangely toward me, though. He's got a crush on Faith and feels she likes me. It's a competition thing." He slowly eased his arm back into his coat sleeve.

Curiosity gnawed at her. "And do you?" Did she really just ask him that at a time like this? *Get a grip, Jay.*

His jaw dropped. "No, not my type." He stood. "Chris is dedicated to saving lives, not taking them."

"So if it's not Dana or Chris, then—"

She gasped and scanned the tree line. "Murdoc is out there watching us and blew it remotely. Probably what drew Herc to the trees."

"Or on a timer. Which means he placed the bomb on our machines while we were at the town hall." Bryson stood. "How would he guess which ones we'd take?"

"This doesn't add up." She gestured toward their broken skis. "I'll call it in. We need help to get back so we can return to Alaska."

He blocked her arm. "Be careful what you say. We can't risk Avery's life."

"I understand." She removed her radio. "Sergeant Park, do you read me?" She waited.

"Go ahead, Jayla."

The man's weakened voice revealed the grief she guessed plagued him over his son's death.

"Need an extraction off Augstone Mountain. Snowmobiles are inoperable." She glanced at the pieces. Inoperable *is an understatement.*

"What's going on? Dana apprised me of the cave they found. She's getting a team ready to investigate further."

"Murdoc took them out. Send a recovery unit to examine the wreckage. We need to get to Alaska. Stat."

"Why?"

She eyed Bryson.

He shook his head.

Time to fabricate an excuse and not tip their hand. "Potential lead."

"Jayla, what aren't you telling me?" Grant asked. "We agreed—no more secrets."

She hated to withhold information from the man who'd taken her under his wing, but she didn't have a choice. "Sorry, sir. Until it pans out, I can't say."

An elongated breath floundered through the radio. "Fine. Sending a team to get you. ETA approximately thirty minutes."

"Thank you, sir."

"Jayla, you know I'd do anything for you. I just wish you'd trust me with whatever you're keeping secret. See you soon."

Tears stung and threatened to spill, but she held them back. She realized keeping the secret was for the best. Avery's life depended on it. She clipped the radio to her waist. "We need to end this. I hate going behind my team's back, especially Grant's."

"We can't trust anyone. It was a mistake sharing everything with the team." Bryson pounded his gloved hand in the snow. "Now Avery's at risk."

"We'll find her."

Bryson's eyes widened. "What if it's a trap and he takes us all out?"

"What do you mean?" Jayla asked.

"You, me and Herc. We're the ones standing in the way of Murdoc's illegal mining ring." Bryson rubbed his arm.

"We can't do this alone, Bry." She lifted her cell phone. "At least let me send these photos to Grant. His unit can dig deep and find something while we're searching for Avery. Something's telling me we're running out of time."

He puffed out a sigh. "Fine. But tell him to keep it top secret. We can't mess this up."

His tone spoke volumes. He wasn't happy with her suggestion.

"Yes, sir." She wondered how the man beside her could be so hot and cold. Earlier, he'd almost kissed her and now... Well, it was probably the last thing on his mind.

Herc nudged close to her, and Jayla kissed his head. "We're leaving soon, bud. I know you're hungry."

Several minutes passed in silence before Bryson took her gloved hand in his. "I'm sorry. I didn't mean to snap at you. Avery's abduction rattled me."

"I get that. I do. She's like a daughter to you." She chewed on her bottom lip. "After everything we've been through, I thought you trusted me." Wait—hadn't he recently asked *her* the same question?

"I do, but—" He averted his gaze.

An earlier comment he'd made resurfaced. "Does this have anything to do with Gabby?"

He flinched, and his narrowed eyes met hers. "How do you know about her?"

From the look on his face, she'd hit a nerve. *There's a story there. Somewhere.* "I don't. Just that you mentioned the name a couple days ago and clammed up when I asked about her. Help me understand what's going on in your mind."

He expelled a long huff. "Gabby's the reason I vowed to remain single. Her betrayal cut too deep." He circled his index finger in the snow, as if trying to collect his thoughts. "I met her my first day on the job as a state trooper. We became friends quickly and then dated. I fell hard, fast. She was everything I was looking for in a woman. Well, at least I *thought* so."

The sun broke through the clouds, sending a ray of hope beaming down on them. Perhaps a sign of things to come? Jayla sent up a silent prayer for Avery.

"We dated for two months before I introduced her to my niece," he continued. "I just didn't want the little girl to get her hopes up. Avery loved her, but Gabby was always reserved. Now I know why. She never cared for anyone but herself. I was blind to that—and five months later, I bought a ring. I was going to propose."

Images of Michael filled her mind. The man she'd planned to marry. Her hand flew to her neck, where her ring still hung on a chain. "I'm sorry. You don't have to explain if you don't want to." She longed to hear his story but also knew the heartache that came from loss.

"Rumors began swirling that I was taking bribes."

Jayla drew in a sharp breath. "What?"

"A couple days later, a fellow trooper found drugs and a wad of cash in my cruiser after he'd received a tip. My father was livid, but I told him someone set me up. He launched an investigation."

"Let me guess—Gabby put them there." Anger flushed her cheeks, and she clenched her teeth to silence the emotion. How could anyone pretend to love someone and betray them like that?

"Yup. Even though our relationship was shaky, my father believed in my innocence, so he dug deeper into all of his officers' lives. He found out that when Gabby worked in Anchorage, there were rumors of another trooper being on the take. She was the common denominator. They exonerated me." He paused. "I decided I didn't want to be a trooper any longer. I'd always loved the wilderness, so I changed vocations."

"What happened to Gabby?"

"We didn't press charges, but Dad fired her. I heard from a fellow acquaintance that she left the state. Relocated out east somewhere but died in a drug-bust-gone-wrong shoot-out. Even after everything she did to me, I grieved her death."

"That's understandable. You loved her. It's difficult to come back from that."

"Avery took it hard, so I vowed to stay single." He fingered his zipper. "But then you came along, and now I'm not sure any longer."

A small, sharp inhale escaped before she could stop it. Questions nagged her. Was this his way of revealing his feelings for her? Had she wanted him to kiss her earlier? Was her heart opening up to this man?

Michael's face flashed before her, and she jumped up. No—she couldn't go there.

"Jayla?"

"I can't—"

Snowmobile engines roared nearby, interrupting the emotions battling inside her.

Help had arrived...just in the nick of time to save her heart from further pain.

Bryson pinched the bridge of his nose, hoping to ward off both the migraine slithering into his head and his frustration from the conversation with Jayla. He had bared everything, but it appeared it was all for nothing. *She doesn't want a relationship. Give it a rest, man.* She had remained silent when they arrived back at her sergeant's station.

She sent the photos to Sergeant Park and asked he keep it a secret.

After a medic looked at Bryson's cut, they left for Alaska. Bryson struggled to stay within the speed limit with Avery's life on the line, but he kept himself in check. He'd restocked his provisions from his station, ensuring his weapon, flashlight, radio, bear spray, flare gun and other supplies were secure on his duty belt. He avoided conversation and left without talking to any of his team.

Bryson gripped his Jeep's steering wheel tighter and turned into the area where Murdoc had said he had Avery. They had checked the coordinates, which took them directly into Bryson's favorite park—but also to the same spot where the grizzly had taken his sister's life. Coincidence? He didn't believe in those. Somehow, Murdoc knew about his family tragedy, which meant Murdoc was someone he knew personally or had members of Bryson's unit working with him. Not that Ellie's attack had been a secret, but it wasn't something his parents or he talked about frequently. He also had disclosed details of Julie's attack to his leader, so the situation became known at his station. That mistake continued to hang over him like a black cloud.

"What do we do now?" Jayla broke the silence radiating between them. "This feels like a trap to me, and I don't want to put us or Herc at risk."

"I understand. But Avery needs me, and Murdoc specifically asked for all three of us to come to the meeting place." He patted his duty belt. "I made sure I included extra ammo."

"Do you have another gun? I practice at a range regularly."

"I do. It's in the back. Let's head out." He climbed out

of his Jeep and retrieved a Glock. He handed it to her. "I have to tell you—this is the area where Ellie died."

She grasped his arm. "Do you feel Murdoc knows you and picked the location on purpose?"

"I do. No way it's a coincidence." Bryson adjusted his belt. "We'll start at the exact camping spot where Ellie's attack happened."

He led them down the trail and soon found where he'd pitched their tents years ago. It had been a popular spot for campers, secluded in the woods and close to a lake.

Bryson ducked under a snow-covered branch and advanced to the spot where his sister had died. Emotions bubbled inside him, threatening to erupt. *Stay strong, Bry. For Avery.* He proceeded, then stopped and sucked in a breath.

Snow had been cleared from the small wooden cross that marked the exact site of his sister's attack. An envelope attached to a string flapped in the breeze.

Murdoc wanted to remind him of the horrific time in his life when Bryson's fear began.

"What is it, Bry?"

He pointed. "Murdoc did this. The snow would have buried the small cross we placed there years ago. He dug it out so I'd see it."

Images of Ellie and the bear charging at Avery flooded his mind, but he pushed them aside.

For Avery.

He must find her. He trudged through the snow and yanked the envelope from the cross, tearing it open.

You'll find sweet Avery in a place where grizzlies lie low for winter. Be quick before Mama bear wakes. Redeem yourself for Ellie and Julie. M

"No!" He thrust the note into Jayla's hand. "Murdoc is playing a sick game at my niece's expense."

Jayla read, her eyes widening. "What? He knows about Julie's attack, too? How?"

"I had to write a report for my boss after it happened. Jayla, Murdoc has to be someone who knows both of our teams."

"But who?"

He gritted his teeth. "I've been racking my brain trying to figure out who has a vendetta against me. The only person I know of is Gabby. She vowed to get even for my dad firing her. Taking Avery would do that."

"Didn't she die?"

"Yes, but she had a half brother. She talked about him often. They were close, but I never met the man."

Jayla handed him back the note. "What location is Murdoc referring to?"

"Bears hibernate in different spots. Trees, dens, under rocks and tree roots, and in—" He stopped.

"Caves," Jayla said.

"Yes, and I'm aware of one near here." Bryson ran, praying as he went. *God, I still don't know if You're real, but I'm begging You. Please protect Avery and all of us. Don't let Murdoc win.* A verse his mother had shared with him lodged in his mind. *He that dwelleth in the secret place of the most High shall abide under the shadow of the Almighty.*

Bryson stopped when he arrived at the cave's entrance and bowed his head.

His mother believed in God's shelter and redemption. Could he? He was tired of trying to redeem himself to everyone around him—including his father. It was time for him to surrender to the One who held him in His hands—

sheltering him from harm. *I see You now, Lord. Forgive me for my unbelief. I surrender and give my life to You. Do with me what You want, but please save Avery.*

A shiver flowed through his body—not from the cold but a wave of peace. God's reassurance that He was there with him. No matter what happened.

"You okay?" Jayla rested her hand on his back.

"Just surrendering to God."

She smiled. "I see it on your face. You have a peace to you."

"I do. Let's bring Avery home." Bryson unleashed his weapon and flashlight from his belt.

Her face wrenched, revealing sadness. "Wait. I'm not going inside a cave with Herc when there could be angry bears. I can't put his life at risk."

A weak cry sounded from inside the cave.

Hercules barked and pulled free of Jayla's hold on him, racing into the dark entrance.

"No!" Jayla yelled, running after him.

Bryson sprinted to reach her and grabbed her hand. "Let me go first." He raised his weapon and flashlight as he entered the cave.

He shined his light around the dark area and stopped at the sight of Avery gagged and tied. Her terror-stricken eyes turned toward something on the opposite wall.

Bryson shined the beam and stopped at a golden brown mass of fur, moving slowly up and down. He gasped and dropped the light. It clattered onto the cave's floor. *Stupid.* The grizzly stirred from its hibernation.

Ruff!

Horror mounted as Bryson's legs weakened, and sweat formed on his forehead despite the cool air. He scooped up the light as a theory zipped through his mind.

Murdoc had them exactly where he wanted them.

In a cave with a bear and a barking dog. It was only a matter of time before the animal awoke fully.

God, show me what to do. Protect Avery!

He turned to Jayla. "Keep Hercules quiet and raise your flashlight to give me light, but don't shine it close to the bear's position." Thankfully, Avery was on the opposite side of the cave from where the grizzly was nestled.

She tugged Hercules's leash. "Hercules, out!"

The dog retreated, obeying his handler's whispered but forceful command.

"What are you going to do?" Jayla raised the beam in Avery's direction.

Bryson tucked his flashlight back into his belt and removed his bear spray—something he always kept on his belt when entering a park. "I'm getting us out of here. Stay perfectly still." He raised the canister in one hand, his gun in the other. He would not shoot the bear unless absolutely necessary. "Squirt, I'm coming. Stay quiet. I've got you." He slowly inched toward them, praying the bear would remain in a stilled state.

He reached Avery and inspected her ropes. She was tied to an ice pick stuck in between two rock formations. No way would he be able to free her without making noise. He kneeled beside her, holstered his weapon and placed the can next to him before removing his multi-tool pocket knife. He flipped the blade open and cut her ropes.

The bear adjusted its position.

Bryson dropped his knife, snatched the canister and lifted Avery in one swift motion. He slowly backed away as he raised the bear spray and held his breath.

Would the animal totally awaken from its hibernated state before they could exit the cave?

Lord, keep it still.

* * *

"Hercules, come!" Jayla's whispered command sounded too loud in the cave. She moved toward the entrance, keeping her Glock aimed at the grizzly. It had stirred at their intrusion but so far hadn't opened its eyes. Jayla muzzled the light's beam and prayed for safety.

The bear changed positions.

Jayla clamped her mouth shut as they exited the cave.

"Quick, let's get back to the Jeep," Bryson said. "Just in case it wakes and comes after us."

"You go first. Get Avery to safety. I'm right behind you." Jayla walked backward in the snow, keeping her weapon trained on the entrance. She wasn't taking any risks.

She reached the tree line and turned. "Hercules, come!" They hustled back to the path and followed Bryson as he carried his sobbing niece down the trail.

They reached the Jeep.

"You drive." Bryson passed Jayla the key fob before placing Avery in the back seat and climbing in beside her.

Jayla opened the passenger door. "Hercules, up."

He hopped onto the seat.

Jayla scooted around to the driver's side and got in, turning to ensure Bryson and Avery were secure.

He untied Avery's gag and kissed her forehead. "You're okay, Squirt. Uncle Bry's got you. Jayla, head to my station." He gave her directions.

Emotion choked in Jayla's throat as she started the engine and peeled out of the parking lot, heading toward Faircord Junction's station.

Five minutes later, she relaxed her snug grip on the wheel. "That was too close."

"Agree," Bryson said. "Murdoc is an evil person to put a child in danger."

"Yes, and he probably thought you'd freeze again, but you didn't. I'm so proud of you for facing your fears." She stole a glimpse over her shoulder.

Avery had snuggled close to Bryson and fallen asleep. Seemed the terror had tired her out.

Bryson kissed his niece's forehead. "God helped me. That's the only answer because He nudged me and gave me strength."

Was he right? Had God heard both of their prayers? She set the question aside and turned her gaze back to the road.

Bryson's cell phone dinged, and he gulped in an audible breath.

"What is it?" Jayla asked.

"Murdoc again. He texted this message. 'Nice job getting away from the grizzly. I underestimated you, but it won't happen again. Next time, you die.'"

Jayla banged on the steering wheel. "We have to figure out who Murdoc is—and fast. This has to end."

"I'm getting Mom and Dad to meet us there. I need them to take Avery to safety while we determine our next steps." He made the call.

Jayla pulled into Bryson's station fifteen minutes later. She parked beside a state trooper cruiser and a metallic-blue SUV.

The Clarkes exited their vehicles.

Jayla unbuckled her seat belt, dropped the keys into her pocket and went to Herc's door. She let him out.

Bryson jumped out from the back seat and lifted Avery, handing her to his mother. "Please take her somewhere off our normal grid until we catch Murdoc."

His mother nodded. "Yes, I'm heading to a friend's cabin."

Bryson turned to his dad. "Can you escort them?"

Another cruiser screamed into the parking lot.

"I have someone ready to do that. I'm staying here with you. We need to figure this mess out, son." Lieutenant Trent Clarke rubbed his granddaughter's back. "We need her safe."

"Agreed." Bryson hugged his mom. "Thank you. Love you."

The scene wrenched Jayla's heart as a sudden desire to be around her family surfaced. "I'll meet you inside, Bry. I need to call Dekker. Hercules, come." She removed her cell phone and entered the station, calling her brother. She walked into the lunchroom for privacy. Herc followed, and she tossed him a treat.

"Hey, Jayla," Dekker said.

Jayla sat at a round table. "How are you feeling?"

"Better, now that I've had a good rest."

She fingered a pen and notepad sitting on the table. "It's so good to hear your voice."

"You sound sad. You okay, sis? Where are you?"

"I'm fine." She squashed the idea of telling him more. He had enough to worry about after getting shot. "I'm in Alaska. Should be back soon."

Her cell chimed, announcing a text. She checked the screen. Sergeant Park sent her and Bryson information about the Warblow Brothers Corporation.

"Listen, the nurse is ordering me to bed," Dekker said. "Gotta run. Please stay safe."

Bryson's and his father's voices sounded in the hallway. "Dad, let's discuss this with Thamesford." He waved to her as they passed by the lunchroom.

She lifted her hand at the pair. "Will do. Love you."

"You, too, sis." He clicked off.

She bent down to pet Herc. "You're a good boy."

Her cell phone rang, and she checked the screen. *Unknown caller.*

She hesitated, then hit Accept. "Hoyt here."

"Jayla?" the weakened voice asked.

She shot out of her chair. She'd know that voice anywhere. "Ethan? You're alive?"

"Barely."

Images of her beloved leader filled her mind. "How?"

"I'll explain when you come get me," Ethan said.

Hope surged through her body. "Where are you?"

He gave her directions to an ice cave on the Alaska border. "Jayla, come alone. Bring Herc. Hurry, before he comes back. Tell. No one. Murdoc has eyes everywhere." He ended the call.

Ethan is alive?

Something niggled at the back of her brain. She picked up the pencil and scribbled on the notepad.

Jayla fished out Bryson's key fob. "Hercules, come."

She had to save her boss before Murdoc got to him. Again.

SEVENTEEN

Bryson left Thamesford's office to search for Jayla. He wanted to talk to her about Sergeant Park's discovery and his father's plan to draw Murdoc out into the open. It was dangerous, but they couldn't think of any other option. Lieutenant Trent Clarke wouldn't put his family at risk any longer, and neither would Bryson. Murdoc and his accomplices had to be taken down. Sergeant Park had discovered the Warblow Brothers Corporation was a front for an illegal ring suspected of smuggling weapons across the border. They obviously were providing easy access to dynamite for Murdoc. The constables were continuing their investigation into the Warblows.

"Son, wait." His dad jogged and caught up to him. "I want to talk to you for a second."

Bryson pulled him into a nearby office. "What's up?"

"I should have told you this a long time ago, but I failed miserably." The older man's normally stoic voice trembled. "Son, I don't blame you for Ellie's death."

What?

"You don't?" Bryson stuffed his hands into his pockets, lost for words.

"I never did, even though I acted like I had." His dad slumped against a wall. "I blamed myself for not being a better father to you and Ellie. My job took me away from you."

Not the words Bryson had expected. "But, Dad, your job is important."

"But I failed you both and Avery. After Avery's father died, I should have been there. I withdrew, as I didn't know how to react to Ellie's grief." He pushed himself off the wall and stood in front of Bryson, towering over him. "But you stepped up and did what I should have."

Bryson clenched his fists. "But I didn't save Ellie. She died on my watch."

Lieutenant Trent Clarke rested his hands on Bryson's shoulders. "It wasn't your fault—just like Gabby's betrayal wasn't. I should have stood up for you more in that situation, too. Son, I haven't told you this enough, but I'm so proud of what you do. Proud of the man you've become." He took a breath. "God is showing me that now. I'm sorry it took me so long to utter those simple words."

Bryson clamped his hands at his sides. If only his father had—

Forgive.

The word interrupted his thought. Where had it come from?

"Wait… You believe in God?" Bryson's whispered question tumbled out.

"I do. Your mother has been a tremendous influence." A smiled tugged at his lips.

Bryson wrapped his arms around his father. "Me, too, Dad. I'm sorry for not being a better son. I'm sorry for failing you."

His father squeezed harder. "Don't say that. You never failed me. Ever."

A tear escaped down Bryson's cheek as years of regret washed over him, cleansing him and giving him a sense of renewal. Redemption. A fresh start. "I love you, Dad."

The lieutenant released him. "Love you, too. Now, go get Jayla, and let's get this plan underway."

"On it." Bryson bounded out of the office and headed to the lunchroom.

"Jayla, we need—" He stopped at the entrance. Empty. Where was she?

He'd seen her on the phone when he passed by the room a few minutes ago on his way to talk to Supervisor Thamesford. They had wanted her opinion on their plan, so he'd left to bring her into the loop. *Odd.*

He raced back down the corridor to check the restroom. Faith exited just as he raised his hand to knock. "Hey, is Jayla in there?"

"Nope. Haven't seen her." The park ranger shoved her hands into her pockets and walked toward the front of the building.

Bryson returned to the lunchroom to see if Jayla had somehow gone back there. Still empty.

He spied a notepad with something scribbled on it and approached the table.

EI @ ice cave
Border

He froze. He recognized Jayla's handwriting from her reports. Was this cryptic message meant for him?

Elimac Ice Cave? Bryson rushed to the window.

His Jeep was gone.

Why would she leave without telling him? She wouldn't. Something was terribly wrong.

"Hey, Faith tells me you're looking for Jayla."

Bryson pivoted at the sound of Ramsay's voice. "Sorry. Didn't hear you come in. Have you seen her? I'm worried."

"I'm sure she's fine."

Bryson held out the notepad. "I don't think so. Look at this. Plus, my Jeep is gone. I need to find her."

Ramsay whipped out a Glock from behind his back. "You're not going anywhere other than into a grave. Murdoc told me it was your time to die."

Bryson forced in a sharp breath and reached for his gun.

Ramsay's eyes narrowed, revealing his evil intent. "Don't even think about it. Pull it out slowly, and set it on the table."

Bryson obeyed.

Ramsay stepped closer. "Now, raise your hands and step away."

Bryson had to buy time for his dad to come in search of him. "Why, Chris? Why are you working for Murdoc? You're supposed to be saving lives, not taking them."

"You don't realize who I am, do you?" He sneered. "I'll give you a hint. My mother's last name before she married my father was Smith."

No way. "*You're* Gabby's half brother?"

"Good guess. I started working here to get revenge for her."

"Why? She was the one who betrayed me!" Bryson lowered his hands.

Ramsay waggled the gun at him. "Get those hands up. She turned reckless after you got her fired, and it eventually led to her death. I needed justice."

"You kidnapped Avery and put her in harm's way with a grizzly, didn't you?" Bryson bit down on the inside of his mouth.

"Of course. I knew about your cowardly fear of bears, so I took advantage of it. Well, I told Murdoc, and he agreed to the idea, as he wanted Jayla here in Alaska for his final showdown. Said she wouldn't escape his net this time."

Bryson lunged forward. "Why you—"

Ramsay waved the gun. "Stay back."

Bryson halted. "What else did you do for Murdoc?"

"Kept tabs on the team's locations, caused the road-block at Elimac Station, put a little extra something in Don's medication to give him seizures—that sort of thing."

Bryson fisted his hands. "So how do you know Murdoc? Who is he?"

"Something Jayla is about to find out. Fast. I met him at a meeting in Canada when I first started with the Cross-Border Mountain Task Force."

Murdoc is Canadian. Bryson glanced at the notepad and a light bulb went off in his head, revealing Murdoc's identity. "EI" didn't stand for Elimac Ice Cave.

Bryson's mind switched to another ice cave on the Alaska–Yukon border. He had to get there fast.

Ramsay removed a suppressor from his pocket and added it onto his Glock 17. "Time for you to die. For Gabby."

Lord, I need to save Jayla from Murdoc. Help!

"Stand down or I'll shoot!" Lieutenant Trent Clarke's voice boomed from the entryway.

Ramsay turned.

It was enough of a distraction for Bryson to act. He plowed into Ramsay's back as the gun fired before it clattered to the floor.

His father dropped his weapon, clutching his arm.

No!

Pounding footfalls followed, and Thamesford appeared with his weapon raised. He kicked Ramsay's Glock to the side before cuffing him. "It's over, Chris."

"Hardly." The medic smirked. "Clarke, you won't reach her in time."

Jayla! He had to get to her.

Bryson dashed to his father's side. "Dad, you okay?"

"I'll be fine. Go find your girl." He took out a key fob with his left hand. "You've got this. I'm proud of you."

Words Bryson had longed to hear from his father.

Words that warmed his heart. "Thanks, Dad. Love you." He snatched the keys and blasted out of the building.

Time to save the woman he loved.

Jayla raised Bryson's Glock and her flashlight simultaneously, tightening her grip as she approached the cave's entrance. She wasn't about to endanger either Herc's or Ethan's lives. Jayla prayed Bryson had understood her message. She couldn't risk anyone else seeing her words, so she abbreviated what she wanted to tell him. Ducking, she entered the ice cave. If it wasn't for her perilous situation, she would explore the magnificent ice deposits. She shined the beam along the walls and ceiling. The breathtaking beauty of glistening crystal sparkled around her.

Coolness permeated off the walls, sending a shudder through her body, as it reminded her of her mother's freezer. Why would Ethan be hiding in an ice cave? She had to find him and get out of this atmosphere fast.

It brought back too many memories.

"Ethan? Where are you?" Her voice bounced off the walls.

"Are you alone?" Ethan asked from the shadows.

"Just me and Herc." Why the secrecy?

Ethan shuffled out from behind a rock to the right of the entrance, holding a lantern.

Dried cuts and bruises peppered his ashen face. He limped forward.

She stuffed the Glock into the back of her ski pants and threw her arms around his neck. "Thank God you're alive." She leaned back and analyzed his appearance. "Are you okay? We thought you were dead."

"I'm fine. Just a little weary from the fall."

Jayla rubbed both of his arms. "What happened? We saw where you fell."

He bent down and ruffled Herc's ears. "Hey, bud. Good to see you, too."

Herc growled, baring his teeth.

Jayla stiffened. Why was her dog reacting to Ethan in that manner?

A question barreled through her mind. "Ethan, tell me what's going on. How did you survive that fall? Why didn't you reach out to me before today?" Something didn't add up.

Once again, Herc growled before barking.

Ethan sneered. "I can't fool you, boy, can I?" He reached into his pocket and removed a gun. "You just wouldn't leave well enough alone. I was hoping to spare your life, but you and Bryson are like Herc here with a bone. Well, your ranger has been taken care of, and now you will pay for getting in my way."

She staggered backward, her pulse pounding in her head as the realization slammed her hard. "You're Murdoc?"

An evil, menacing smile formed on his lips. "You got it."

Heat burned her cheeks despite the cool cave as the betrayal of the man she'd assumed cared for her bubbled to the surface. "What did you do to Bryson?"

"Not me. I have a member from each team on my side. Chris messaged me and said he was about to kill Bryson." He waved the gun in her face. "And you're the last loose end."

Lord, protect Bry. His face popped into her head as a sob stuck in her throat. Suddenly, the idea of never seeing him again sent waves of despair throughout her.

She had to stop her precious leader. "You will not get

away with this. Others are onto you." She casually brought her right hand behind her to retrieve the Glock.

"Keep your hand where I can see it." He circled her and yanked the weapon from the back of her pants. "No one is going to stop me from building my empire. There's a ton of copper ore in these mountains. I'm surprised it took this long for anyone to find it."

"Tell me why. Why betray everyone around you?" Her voice quivered. "You were like an older brother to me. Is this all some stupid get-rich-quick scheme?"

A softened expression passed over his warped face for a split second. "I'm sick, Jayla. I have a rare form of cancer, and I'm undergoing costly experimental treatments. Thankfully, I caught it in good time."

Her jaw dropped. "What? Why go through all this, though? Why didn't you reach out to those who love you? We would have helped."

"You don't have this kind of money. When I stumbled upon copper ore deposits and discovered they weren't catalogued, the idea struck me. I found a silent partner, and we made a deal—I'd mark any copper caves for them to mine during warmer months, and they'd pay me."

Sergeant Park's text now made sense. "Let me guess. The Warblow brothers?"

"Smart girl. However, the dear brothers decided they'd cut me out, so I was planning on killing them."

She pictured the letter from his backpack. "So the strange block-letter note I found in your bag was meant for them?"

"Yes."

She crossed her arms. "How did you fake your death? I saw the avalanche take you."

"That was tricky. My Canadian partner triggered the avalanche. I pushed Hopkins out of the way because he was close to the crevasse I was going to disappear into. Thankfully, it was long enough to catch it further down the mountain. I left my ski and backpack there for you to find."

"But how did you get out?"

"My partner helped me climb out after you guys left." He snickered. "It was a brilliant plan, until you and Bryson started getting suspicious of the avalanches. We had to stop people from finding our caves. We'd mark them and come back to them after things settled."

"'We'? If Chris was your American partner, who's your Canadian one?"

"Philip."

"What? Wait—he blew up the kennel, didn't he?" She dug her fingernails into her palms. He'd put his dogs at risk?

"At my request. And to divert suspicion, he set fire to the safe house. He also hired the female assassin to take out good ole Johnny."

She drew in a sharp breath. "Why would he do that?"

"Why do you think? Money. He sustained injuries in an accident a few years back and got hooked on painkillers. He hid it well, but it eventually turned into a habit he couldn't afford. He was the perfect person to help me."

Remorse filled Jayla. How had she missed her coworker's pain? She would have tried to help. However, it still didn't excuse his behavior. Another question rose. "Ethan, why did you kidnap Hercules?"

"I contracted thugs to do that. You'd be surprised what money can buy. I needed to scare you into feeling your dogs were a target, especially Herc. I hoped it might stop you, but you just wouldn't let it go." He clucked his tongue. "I was going to let him go after one final mining expedition."

"How could you put your life before others after all you

stood for on the Cross-Border Mountain Task Force? You were our leader. We looked up to you." Her heated tone boomed in the cave. She balled her hands into fists and stomped forward.

Herc nudged against her legs. He sensed her anger, too.

He raised the gun higher. "Stay there. Jay, dear, things change after you're given a death sentence. I wanted to live, and it was the only way out of my situation. The treatments are working." He paused. "I only need a bit more money for a final session, and then I'm moving somewhere tropical. No one will ever know."

Jayla bit her lip to stop the pending tears. "I thought I knew you. You helped me through a hard time after I joined the team. I had struggled to redeem myself after my mistakes in the military. You said you understood and mentored me. Was that all an act, too?"·

"Of course not. I do care for you, sweet Jayla—but like I said earlier, facing death changes things."

"Not in a good way for you." Multiple escape scenarios sped through her mind. "What are you going to do to me? People will wonder what happened, especially Sergeant Park."

"Don't you worry, I've got it covered. No one will come looking for you." He pulled a stick of dynamite from his pocket. "Time for you to get locked into a different freezer. This time, your mother won't be around to save you."

No! She couldn't go through that again.

Herc whimpered, reminding her of his presence.

"Please, take Herc with you. Let him live." The idea of her beloved dog freezing to death crushed her heart.

Ethan moved to the entrance, keeping his gun raised. "No way. You have an unbreakable bond in life…and in death." He pocketed the gun and flicked a lighter, igniting the shortened fuse.

Herc growled and inched forward.

Ethan unleashed the gun again and fired into the cave at their feet. "Stay, Herc."

The dog yelped and scrambled backward.

"Don't try looking for another way out. There isn't one." He threw the stick of dynamite in the entrance and backed away but kept his gun raised. "Sorry it came to this, but you shouldn't have interfered. Goodbye, dear Jay."

Once the flame reached the top of the wick, Ethan ran.

Jayla yanked her dog farther away from the opening, sheltering him.

The explosion rocked the cave, sending pounding ice chunks downward and blocking them inside a freezer of death.

Not again, Lord. Please save us. I don't want to die.

Especially since she never got to tell Bryson how she really felt about him.

She hugged Herc close and rocked. "At least I'm not alone this time. I'm sorry I couldn't save you, bud." Another time she'd put someone she loved in harm's way. She hadn't acted quick enough to save Michael from being captured and tortured. Now her dog would die because of her.

He licked her face and nudged her.

She sobbed into Herc's fur.

Trust.

The word rushed through her mind, steeling her jaw. Where had the simple but complex word come from? Was God asking her to come back to Him? Yes, it was time. If she was going to die, she must ask forgiveness and surrender—completely.

Lord, I can't do this alone. I know now You hear me when I cry out to You. I'm sorry for all the times I tried to prove myself with others when, in fact, You were the One who mattered. You're the only redemption I need.

I'm worthy in Your sight, aren't I? She smiled. *Forgive me. Take my life—however long it is—and use it for Your glory. I love You.*

Warmth flowed through her body even though she was locked in an ice cave. She cuddled closer to Herc, letting God's love envelop her.

She wasn't sure how long she'd been sitting there, frozen in God's embrace, when shouts sounded from outside.

Jayla bolted upright. "Help!"

Herc barked.

"Jayla! Where are you?"

She sucked in a breath.

Bryson was alive.

She dashed to the entrance. "Bryson! We're in here. Please save us!"

God had heard her desperate cry and sent the man she loved to set her free.

Bryson listened to determine where Jayla's voice was coming from. He had raced to get to the ice cave, but someone had blocked the entrance to the park. Bryson guessed it had been Ethan—aka Murdoc. "Where are you, Jayla?"

Hercules barked excessively. He was leading Bryson to them.

Bryson quickly radioed his dad and gave him their location before plowing through the snow in the dog's direction, his backpack and equipment slamming into his back. He had grabbed it from his father's trunk and stuffed everything he thought he'd need—ice pick, shovel, flare gun, airbag, beacon. Tools a ranger or mountain-survival specialist never left without, especially in the winter on a mountain.

Bryson stopped when he spotted a pile of ice rocks and

snow blocking the entrance. Murdoc had locked her in—making her face her fears like he had Bryson.

He unhooked the small shovel from his backpack. "I'm here, Jayla."

"Hurry, Ethan's getting away," her muffled yell sounded behind the wall of snow and ice.

Bryson dug as fast as he could. He only needed to penetrate a small opening for them to crawl through, but it seemed like an eternity before he made any type of progress.

"I see light, Bry!" Jayla said. "You're almost to us."

He continued to pick away at the barricade, moving the snow and ice boulders away.

Fifteen minutes later, Jayla and Hercules crawled out of their prison.

He tossed his shovel aside and threw his arms around her. "I'm so glad I found you. I thought I'd lost you."

"Thank you for saving us. God answered my prayer."

"He answered both of ours." He pulled back. "Where's Ethan?"

She pounded her fist on his chest. "I can't believe he fooled me. I trusted him."

"They fooled us all. Which way did Ethan go?"

"I don't know, but we need to get back down the mountain to safety."

"Right. I gave Dad our location, and he and Thamesford are sending help." He radioed for an update. Thamesford revealed they were just around the corner and would be there within minutes.

Bryson picked up the shovel and the open backpack. The flare gun fell out and landed in the snow with a thud.

Jayla picked it up and stuffed it into her pocket. "Wow, you came prepared."

"Ranger's motto." He caressed her face. "I have lots I

want to say to you—but first, let's get to the cruiser and out of the cold."

"You're not going anywhere."

Bryson stiffened and turned at the menacing voice.

Ethan stood at the tree line. "You two just won't die. Well, you can't outrun an avalanche." He held up a device and pressed a button.

The mountain ridge exploded directly above them, followed by a whumping sound as the driving snow rained down on them.

Bryson shoved Jayla, sending her away from the path.

But not in time for him to get out of the snow's trajectory.

It pounded on top of him, bulldozing him down the slope and burying him alive.

His world went dark as a prayer uttered from his lips. *God, save Jayla.*

"Avalanche! Hercules, cover!" Jayla landed in a pile of snow after Bryson had shoved her out of the way, but not before the snow buried him. *Lord, keep Bryson safe. Let Herc be okay so he can find him.*

Beside her, she didn't miss the loud snicker coming from Ethan. He'd stayed in the shadows but obviously wanted to ensure they both died this time.

However, he hadn't counted on Bryson sacrificing himself for Jayla. Something Ethan wouldn't have done. Maybe the old Ethan, but certainly not the new one.

Jayla had to get Hercules looking for Bryson before his air was gone. "Hercules—"

"Not happening, Herc." Ethan raised his gun. "I never wanted to kill a dog, but he can't find Bryson. It's over." His finger twitched on the trigger.

"No!" Jayla remembered what was hiding in her pocket

and she didn't hesitate. She whipped out the flare gun and fired.

The round exploded into Ethan, sending him falling backward into the snow. His body stilled.

Tears stung as her hand shook, and she dropped the flare gun. *Why, Ethan? Why did you make me do it?*

Herc barked, reminding her of Bryson buried by a ton of snow. She turned to him. "Hercules, search!"

The dog cannonballed through the snow, searching for signs of Bryson.

"Come on! I can't lose him." Jayla held her breath as Herc continued his hunt.

Minutes later, her K-9 buried his head into the snow, digging as his tail spiraled in the air.

Jayla raced to Herc's side and dropped to her knees, digging in the same spot. Moments later, she found Bryson's arm. She dug around until she located his head and brushed the snow from his face, clearing all obstructions from his airway before checking his pulse. He was alive but not breathing.

Jayla gave him five rescue breaths, then waited.

He coughed and opened his eyes.

"You're okay. Hercules found you." She dug away more snow so he could break free.

Bryson gasped for breath. "Ethan?"

"Shot him with a flare." She glanced at her former beloved leader lying in the snow. "He's gone. No one points a gun at my dog." She tousled Herc's ears and kissed his forehead. "Good boy."

Herc barked and licked Bryson's face, tail wagging.

"I've never been so glad to have sloppy dog kisses." Bryson eased himself into a seated position. "I need to tell you something."

She placed her gloved index finger on his lips. "Later. When we're sitting beside a fireplace."

Sirens wailed at the mountain's base. Help had arrived.

An hour later, Jayla sat beside Bryson on the couch at the Clarke home. Herc lay curled up on a mat. The fireplace heated her chilled bones, but it was the man cuddled next to her who sent warmth throughout her body. She realized now that the ice around her heart had melted. Time to set aside her fear of falling in love after losing Michael. Who was she kidding?

She already loved Bryson, but the question remained...

Would he accept her after he discovered the secret she'd hidden?

She tensed.

"What is it, Jayla?" He caressed her cheek. "Tell me what's holding you back."

She lifted the chain out from around her neck and raised the diamond ring. "This is the reason I vowed never to get involved with anyone again." She paused. "To make a long story short, I met Michael in the army. We fell in love. He proposed. I said yes. Seems simple, right? However, it didn't prove to be after I botched a mission that resulted in his capture and torture."

Bryson winced. "What happened?"

"I was driving, and he was in the back seat with our unit." She dropped the necklace holding the ring and drew her knees to her chest. "I had trusted false intel and taken a back road. They were waiting for us and launched an RPG. I saw it and lurched the wheel to the right, missing it, but we slammed into a ditch." A tear spilled down her cheek.

Bryson wiped it away. "I'm so sorry. It's not your fault."

"That's not the bad part. After we escaped the blast, we were attacked. We fought some off, but one knocked me unconscious. When I woke up, Michael was gone and the others were dead. I was the only one who survived." She sobbed, the images still fresh in her mind.

Bryson drew her closer. "He was captured?"

"Yes. After days of extensive searching, we found him in an abandoned warehouse. The team rescued him, but not before he was brutally tortured." She gathered her strength. "He was never the same. I soon realized he'd never return to the army. His medical condition allowed him to get discharged. I also knew I couldn't continue, and I gave my notice, knowing I was giving up a lot. I had served many years, and they tried hard to keep me. But I just couldn't do it."

Jayla shifted her position before continuing. "I relocated him to the mountains, hoping it would help him get over whatever had happened in that warehouse. He wouldn't tell me. I figured reliving it would kill him all over again, so I let him tell me in his time. That never happened."

Bryson tucked a blanket over her shoulders. "Counseling didn't help lessen his agony?"

"No. I came over to visit him at the center, and that's when I found him." She let out a long breath. "He'd locked his doors and then hung himself. I'll never forget that scene as long as I live."

"I'm so sorry."

"His death was my fault. I failed him." Once again, she sobbed.

"Sweet Jay. Stop blaming yourself." He hugged her tight. "I've realized Ellie's death wasn't my fault. You have to do the same."

"I know. You're right. I finally surrendered everything to God on the mountain. I've tried so hard to prove myself worthy after Michael's death, but God showed me in the cave He's the only redemption I need." She sat upright, turning to face him. "I've also realized something else."

He stared into her eyes. "What's that?"

"I can't stop my feelings for you, no matter how hard I've tried. You melted the ice around my heart." She traced her index finger along his stubbled chin. "I've fallen in love with you, Ranger Bryson Clarke. Where do—"

He pulled her closer and smothered her lips with his, silencing her question.

The fire crackled, adding to the romantic atmosphere as their kiss lingered.

Hercules barked and burrowed his nose between them.

Bryson laughed. "I love you, too, Jayla Hoyt."

Jayla smiled and leaned back against the couch, snuggling with the two males in her life. Contentment washed over her as a saying her mother had said to her years ago bubbled to the surface.

God always hears us and rewards His children with the desires of their hearts. It just may not be what we had expected, but He knows best.

EPILOGUE

Seven months later

Jayla followed Avery and Bryson to the Ogilwyn Mountain Pass as the golden sun kissed the horizon, sending gorgeous rays illuminating the sky and reminding her of God's majesty. Herc brushed against her legs. Jayla shut her eyes and breathed in the late-summer air. She loved the mountains in every season. Each one brought its own uniqueness to the magnificent ambience, and Jayla couldn't think of anywhere else she'd want to be right now. The man she loved was by her side, with a precious girl leaning against his legs. Plus, Herc rounded out the family she wanted to spend the rest of her life with. Her life was complete. She fingered the cross pendant around her neck. She had released her guilt over Michael's death and replaced his engagement ring with the symbol of her recommitment to Christ. Letting Michael go had been difficult, but God and Bryson had helped her overcome her insecurities.

Ethan Ingersoll had passed away from the flare gun shot. Chris and Philip were facing multiple charges for their crimes. The Warblow brothers had retained an expensive lawyer and were claiming innocence, but Jayla knew better. They had not only supplied Ethan with the dynamite but had also funded his expedition of marking the caves. Local authorities had rounded up Ethan's hired thugs, including the female assassin. The illegal copper-mining ring in the Ogilwyn Pass had been dismantled, and once again peace reigned in their mountains.

Bryson and his father had long talks as they both worked through their guilt from Ellie's death. Their relationship came out stronger, and they'd spent many hours together fishing on their favorite lake. Jayla had vowed to herself to become a better sister to all of her siblings and a better daughter to her parents by reaching out more often.

Sergeant Park had promoted her to the leader of Carimoose Bays Cross-Border Mountain Task Force. Their work on rebuilding a station was well underway, but the question remained. Where would Jayla and Bryson's relationship take them? She was content with either Alaska or the Yukon, as long as they remained in the mountains. It was where they both longed to stay.

"I love every season on top of Ogilwyn." Jayla gazed at the peaks across from them.

"Me too." Bryson held her hand tight. "Do you think I should tell Avery now?"

Jayla turned and stared into his blue eyes. "I do."

"Tell me what, Uncle Bry?" Avery asked, her face brightening.

Bryson squatted in front of her. "I'm adopting you. You're going to be my daughter, Avery Clarke."

She squealed, her eyes widening. "Really?"

"Really."

Avery wrapped her arms around him. "I love you, Daddy. Can I call you that now?"

Bryson let out an audible gasp at the little girl's use of *Daddy*. "Of course. Love you, too, Squirt."

She stepped back. "Is it time?"

What did that mean?

Bryson nodded and pulled a box from his pocket, then bent down on one knee. But instead of opening it, he handed it to Avery and winked.

She held it out to Jayla, lifting the cover. "Will you be my mama?" An ear-to-ear grin exploded on her sweet face.

Jayla's jaw dropped. "Is this your way of proposing, Bry?"

He plucked out the ring. "It sure is. I love you with all my heart, Jayla Hoyt. Will you marry me?"

She dropped to her knees. "Yes! Yes! Yes!"

Avery giggled. "That's a lot of yeses."

Jayla chuckled and held Bryson's face in her hands, tugging him closer. "I love you, too, my prince." She kissed his lips.

"Ew," Avery said. "Put the ring on, Daddy."

Hercules barked and nestled between Jayla and Bryson, breaking their hold.

"See, Herc agrees." Avery jumped up and down. "Come on!"

Jayla held out her hand. "Yeah, Daddy." She snickered.

Bryson slid the ring snug on her finger and hauled her up to her feet.

"Show her the other present." Avery danced a circle around them.

"You mean there's more?" Jayla's throat clogged at the thought of anything else.

Bryson retrieved his cell phone from his pocket and swiped the screen. "This is my wedding present to you."

She tilted her head, a smile twitching. "So you *were* expecting me to say yes?"

He raised a brow as his lips tilted upward, turning his grin into a dance. "Bertie told me you would."

"Bertie?"

"I've gone back to visit him many times. He's the one who mentioned this." He turned the phone in her direction. "It's ours."

Jayla leaned in for a better look and covered her mouth with both hands to contain her excitement. Could it be true?

The image of a log-style ranch resting at the foot of a mountain and at the edge of a lake stared back at her.

Her dream home. "You bought this? Where is it?"

"On the Alaska–Yukon border. Right in the middle of both our stations. The perfect solution to all our discussions."

Herc barked.

"Yes, the perfect spot for you, too, bud." Bryson tousled the dog's ears. "What do you think, Jay?"

"I absolutely love it, and I love you." She squealed and launched herself into his arms. She pushed back and studied his handsome face. "You are a treasure from God."

A golden-crowned sparrow trilled its three-note song as if in agreement before it fluttered off into the distance.

Jayla smiled and leaned against Bryson, staring at the horizon as the sun rose higher, bringing a spectacular yellow-orange display.

And hope for a better tomorrow filled with promises.

God had listened to her prayers, saved her from wickedness and brought her back from the abyss, clearly revealing her worthiness. After all, she was His workmanship, and she'd praise Him forever.

From the mountaintop.

* * * * *

If you liked this story from Darlene L. Turner,
check out her previous Love Inspired Suspense books:

Border Breach
Abducted in Alaska
Lethal Cover-Up
Safe House Exposed
Fatal Forensic Investigation
Explosive Christmas Showdown

Available now from Love Inspired Suspense!
Find more great reads at www.LoveInspired.com.

Dear Reader,

Thank you for reading Jayla, Bryson and Hercules's story! The golden retriever is named after the incredible Hercules aircraft used to provide relief to those in need. As well, its search and rescue role seemed like the perfect fit for my lifesaving Hercules. Jayla and Bryson both battled with proving their worth but in the end realized God's redemption was there all along. We can all learn from their journey. Also, there are times we feel God doesn't hear our prayers, but He's listening. We only need to be still and wait.

I enjoyed creating the fictional joint US/Canadian Cross-Border Mountain Task Force and the Ogilwyn Mountain Pass that stretches from the Yukon into Alaska.

I'd love to hear from you. You can contact me through my website, www.darlenelturner.com, and also sign up for my newsletter to receive exclusive subscriber giveaways. Thanks for reading my story.

God bless,
Darlene L. Turner

SHIELDING THE BABY
Pacific Northwest K-9 Unit • by Laura Scott

Following his sister's murder, former army medic Luke Stark becomes the next target when someone attempts to kidnap his son. K-9 officer Danica Hayes and her K-9 are determined to keep Luke and his child safe while unmasking the culprit...before it's too late.

AMISH WILDERNESS SURVIVAL
by Mary Alford

To find her missing brother, Leora Mast must first survive the danger that followed her to Montana. She finds an unexpected ally in Fletcher Shetler...but unraveling the truth behind her brother's disappearance will be harder than she ever imagined. Can they stay alive long enough to save her brother?

TARGETED IN THE DESERT
Desert Justice • by Dana Mentink

After recovering from a murder attempt, Felicia Tennison receives an anonymous message that she has a secret younger sister...and her life is at risk. Now she needs help from ex-boyfriend Sheriff Jude Duke while they seek answers—and dodge deadly attacks.

YOSEMITE FIRESTORM
by Tanya Stowe

Park ranger Olivia Chatham and search-and-rescue leader Hayden Bryant lead a group of climbers to safety from a raging inferno in Yosemite, but killers have orders to destroy all witnesses to their crime...including Olivia. Can Olivia and Hayden get to safety before the flames and killers get to them?

MISTAKEN MOUNTAIN ABDUCTION
by Shannon Redmon

With her twin abducted and mistaken for her, former army lieutenant Aggie Newton must figure out why she's become a target. Together, Aggie and Detective Bronson Young search for answers and her sister, but the kidnappers will do anything to end their investigation.

WYOMING COLD CASE SECRETS
by Sommer Smith

When Brynn Evans learns she was adopted as an infant, she begins digging into her past...and finds a killer intent on stopping her. Brynn's mysterious background is just the kind of challenge private investigator Avery Thorpe can't resist, but is revealing old secrets worth their lives?

HARLEQUIN
PLUS

Try the best multimedia subscription service for romance readers like you!

Read, Watch and Play.

Experience the easiest way to get the romance content you crave.

Start your **FREE TRIAL** at
www.harlequinplus.com/freetrial.